Clare Connelly was raised in small-town Australia among a family of avid readers. She spent much of her childhood up a tree, Harlequin romance book in hand. Clare is married to her own real-life hero and they live in a bungalow near the sea with their two children. She is frequently found staring into space—a surefire sign she is in the world of her characters. She has a penchant for French food and ice-cold champagne, and Harlequin novels continue to be her favorite-ever books. Writing for Harlequin Presents is a long-held dream. Clare can be contacted via clareconnelly.com or on her Facebook page.

Books by Clare Connelly

Harlequin Presents

Innocent in the Billionaire's Bed
Bought for the Billionaire's Revenge
Her Wedding Night Surrender

Visit the Author Profile page
at Harlequin.com for more titles.

To my fabulous South Australian Romance Association friends: smart, supportive and kind women who sparkle like ornaments all year round.

Clare Connelly

BOUND BY THEIR CHRISTMAS BABY

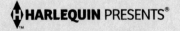
HARLEQUIN PRESENTS®

Recycling programs
for this product may
not exist in your area.

ISBN-13: 978-1-335-50489-0

Bound by Their Christmas Baby

First North American publication 2018

Printed in U.S.A.

www.Harlequin.com

He was going to kiss her, and she was going to let him. Heck, she was going to kiss him if he took much longer.

"What is that?"

The question surprised her, almost as much as when he pulled away from her and looked around, bewildered.

It took a few more seconds for Abby to hear what he had.

"Raf!" She shot him a look of frustration and sanity began to seep back in. She had no business wanting to kiss this man, let alone while their child was screaming from the bedroom.

In the seconds it took her to compute the situation, Gabe was already moving to the hallway. He pushed into the bedroom and stood there, staring at the crib as though he'd never seen a baby in his entire life.

"Excuse me," Abby said, shifting past him to scoop Raf up.

"What is this?" he asked, finally, dumbfounded.

"What do you think?"

"It's a baby."

She could have laughed, it was so absurd. "Yes, it's a baby. This is your son."

Christmas Seductions

When seduction leads to diamond rings...

Billionaire foster brothers, and business partners, Gabe Arantini and Noah Moore have no intention of settling down anytime soon—they're notorious bachelors and they intend to keep it that way. That is until they each meet their match!

As they embark on forbidden Christmas seductions they find for the first time they've met their match! With the festivities in the air, could these two bachelors change their ways, starting with a diamond ring for their ladies?

Find out what happens in:

Noah's story
The Season to Sin

Available in Harlequin Dare

Gabe's story
Bound by Their Christmas Baby

Available in Harlequin Presents

CHAPTER ONE

GABE WAS BORED. He always was at these damned things, but they were part and parcel of his life. His job. His all. And he'd never been a man to walk away from a challenge.

God knew Noah—his business partner and best friend—wasn't going to step forward to attend a damned investors' dinner. A party in a club, sure. Noah would be there in an instant. But this kind of entertaining fell to Gabe, and Gabe alone. He looked around the table, smiling blandly, wondering how much more he had to endure before he could make his excuses and leave.

There were a thousand better ways than this to spend an evening.

He hadn't been to New York in a year, and the last time? Well, it had been a spectacular disaster. No wonder he'd avoided it like the plague. Too much melancholy at Christmas, that was the problem. He'd actually allowed himself to feel lonely, to feel alone, to feel sorry for himself. That was why he'd been stupid enough to fall for her ploy.

'Calypso's going to be game-changing,' Bertram Fines said with confidence. 'You've done it again.'

Gabe ignored the flattery. People were all too

quick with praise now that he and Noah had established the foremost technology company in the world. It was the early years when they'd been without friends, without funds, and still made it work through sheer perseverance and determination. He reached for his glass. It was empty. He lifted a hand in the air, summoning a waiter without lifting his gaze.

'This is the culmination of a lot of innovation, and even more research. Calypso isn't just a smartphone, it's a way of life,' he said with a lift of his shoulders. It was the culmination of an idea he and Noah had years earlier, and they'd worked tirelessly to get it to this point—almost to the market. Calypso went beyond the average smartphone. It was smarter. More secure, guaranteeing its users more privacy.

His spine straightened with a *frisson* of alarm when he recalled how close he'd come, a year ago, to compromising the project. How close he'd come to seeing Calypso's secrets taken to one of his business rivals.

But that hadn't eventuated. He'd made sure of that. His eyes glinted with the ferocity of his thoughts, the strength of his resentment, but his smile was all wolf-like charm.

'How can I help you, sir?' A woman appeared to his left. A brassy redhead with a pleasing figure and a smile that showed she knew it. Once upon a time, Gabe might have smiled back. Hell, he'd have done more than smile back—he'd have laid on the charm, asked what time she finished her shift, and then he'd have seduced her. Bought her a drink, taken her for a drive in his limousine before inviting her to his hotel room.

But the last time he'd done that, he'd learned his lesson. He would never again invite a wolf in sheep's clothing to his bed, nor a woman dressed like a temptress who'd come to betray him. Before he had met Abigail Howard, Gabe couldn't have imagined going a month without the company of a beautiful woman between his sheets, but now it had been a year. A year since Abigail, a year without women, and he barely cared.

He named a bottle of wine, one of the most expensive on the menu, without smiling, and turned his attention back to his table of guests. Conversation had moved onto the cost of midtown realty. He sat back, pretending to listen, fingers in a temple beneath his chin.

The restaurant was quietening down. Despite the fact it was one of Manhattan's oldest and most prestigious spots, it was late—nearing midnight—and the conservative crowd that favoured this sort of establishment were wrapping up their evenings.

Gabe let his eyes run idly around the room. It was everything he'd come to expect in this kind of place, from the glistening chandeliers that sparkled overhead to the sumptuous burgundy velvet curtains adorning the windows, to the menu and wine list that were both six-star.

The waitress approached with the wine and he gestured that she should fill up his companions' glasses. For Gabe's part, he wasn't a big drinker, and certainly not with men he hardly knew. Discretion was the better part of valour—another lesson he'd learned a year ago. No, that wasn't true. He'd known it all his life. She'd just made him forget.

His eyes wandered once more, this time towards the kitchens, concealed behind large white doors that flapped silently as staff moved quickly through them. Inside, he knew, would be a hive of activity, despite the calm serenity of the restaurant dining room. The doors flicked open and for the briefest moment Gabe was certain he saw her.

A flick of white-blonde hair, a petite figure, pale skin.

He gripped the stem of his empty wine glass, his whole body stilled, like a predator on alert.

It wasn't her. Of course it wasn't.

In the kitchen? Had that been a dishcloth in her hand?

Not possible.

He homed back in on the conversation at the table, laughing at a joke, nodding at something someone said, but every few moments his eyes shifted towards the doors, trying to get a better look at the ghost of Christmas last.

Gabe wasn't a man to leave things to chance. He'd experienced enough random acts, enough of fate's whimsy, to know that he would never again let life surprise him.

She had surprised him though, that night. What was it about the woman that had got under his skin? She was beautiful, but so were many women, and Gabe wasn't a man who let a woman's appearance overpower him. In fact, he prided himself on being more interested in a woman's mind. Her intellect. The decency of her soul and conscience.

And yet she'd walked into the bar of his Manhattan hotel and their eyes had sparked. Then he'd held his breath for the longest time, waiting for her to say something, needing to hear her voice and to know all about her instantly.

What madness had overtaken him that night?

It hadn't been a random spark though. Their meeting had been planned meticulously. He forced himself to return his attention to his guests, but his mind was on that long-ago night, a night he usually tried not to remember. A night he would never forget. Not because it had been so wonderful—though at the time he thought it had been—but because of the lessons it had taught him.

Don't trust anyone. Ever. Except for Noah, Gabe

was alone in this world, and that was the way he wanted it.

Still, the mystery of the vision of Abby remained, so that, as the night wore on and cars were called for the investors, he gestured towards the maître d'.

'How has your evening been, Mr Arantini?' the man asked with an obsequious bow. Gabe might have grown up dirt-poor, but he'd been phenomenally wealthy for a long time now; such marked deference was not new to him. He'd even come to find it amusing.

Gabe didn't answer the question. There was no need. If he hadn't found the evening a success, the maître d' would have heard about it well before then. 'I'd like to speak to Rémy,' he said silkily.

'The chef?'

Gabe lifted a brow. 'Unless you have two Remys working this evening.'

The maître d' laughed a little self-consciously. 'Not at all, sir. Just the one.'

'Then I'll let myself into the kitchen.' He stood and spun on his heel, stalking towards the doors without allowing the maître d' a reply.

At the doors, though, he hesitated for the briefest moment, bracing himself for the likelihood that he might come face to face with her once more. And the greater likelihood that he would not.

So?

Why did that bother him?

If he'd wanted to see Abigail Howard again, he'd had ample opportunities. She'd called him relentlessly, desperate to 'apologise' for her part in the scam. Desperate to see him, to make amends. Didn't she realise how futile those efforts were? As if Gabe could ever forgive such a betrayal! He'd left her in little doubt as to how he felt when she'd turned up at his office in Rome—for heaven's sake—demanding to see him.

That had been six months ago. Six months after she'd bargained her innocence for a glimpse at top secret Calypso files on behalf of her father. His blood still curdled at what that night had been about—at what she'd been willing to give up for commercial success.

He'd known a lot of manipulative characters in his time, but none so abhorrent as she'd been.

The satisfaction of having his security remove her from his office had been immense. She'd come to Rome to see him and he'd made it painstakingly obvious that he'd never see her again.

So? What was he doing now? Hovering outside a restaurant kitchen because he thought he'd caught a glimpse of her? And how could he possibly have recognised her in the brief moment the blonde had walked past the doors? It wasn't physically possible, he told himself, all the while knowing he *had* recognised something about the woman. The lithe grace of her walk. The elegance of her neck as she turned her head, hair that was like clouds at sunset, glowing with the evening's rays.

Great.

Now he was becoming poetic about a woman who'd seduced him with the sole intention of ruining him.

He tightened his shoulders and pushed into the kitchen. It wasn't so busy as he'd thought earlier. The dinner rush was over, and now there were chefs prepping for the next day's service, some cleaning, some standing around talking. His eyes skimmed the kitchen and his stomach dropped unexpectedly.

She wasn't here. This was a men-only zone at present—something he'd never allow in any of his hotels or restaurants. Within his and Noah's company, Bright Spark Inc, they demanded equal gender representation across the board. They invested heavily in STEM projects for schools—they were both passionate about playing fields being levelled as much as possible, having been on the dodgy end of their own playing fields for a long time.

'Rémy,' he said smoothly, striding across the kitchen.

'Ah! Arantini!' The chef grinned. 'You like your dinner?'

'Exceptional.' Gabe nodded, annoyingly put out

by having come into the kitchens and not found the woman he'd seen.

'You had the lobster?'

'Of course.'

'Always your favourite,' Rémy chuckled.

Gabe nodded, just as the cold room door opened and the woman stepped out. Her head was bent, but he'd have known her body anywhere, any time and in any clothes.

True, the night they'd met she'd been dripping in the latest couture, but now? She wore simple jeans, a black T-shirt and a black and white apron tied twice around her slender waist. Her hair was pulled into a ballerina bun and her face, he saw as she lifted it, was bare of make-up.

His gut twisted and a strong possessive instinct hammered through him.

She'd been his in bed. That hadn't been just about Calypso. She'd wanted him. She'd given him her virginity, she'd begged him to take her, and he'd thought it a gift. A special, beautiful moment. He'd never been anyone's 'first' before.

She placed the containers she was carrying onto the bench and then lifted her eyes to the clock above the doors. She hadn't seen him, and he was glad for that. Glad to have a moment to observe her, to remember all the reasons he had for hating this woman, to regain his composure before showing her how little he thought of her.

When he'd had her evicted from his office in Rome, he'd told himself it was for the best. He never wanted to see her again, and nothing could change that. But here, in this six-star Manhattan hotspot, looking nothing like his usual romantic quarry, Gabe knew he'd been lying to himself.

He'd wanted to see her again and again. He drank in the sight of her, knowing it could only ever be this minute, this weakness, this moment of indulgence, before he would be forced to remember that she'd planned to ruin him.

Bright Spark Inc wasn't just a business to him. It was his and Noah's life. It had saved them when their own futures had been bleak and they'd been desperate for a fresh start.

And she'd wanted to destroy it. She'd come to him specifically to steal Calypso's secrets. It was a crime for which there could never be sufficient repentance.

'Rémy.' He spoke deliberately, slowly, and loud enough that she heard. He had the satisfaction of seeing her head jerk towards him the moment the word was uttered, saw shock flood her huge, expressive green eyes, saw the colour drain from her face and the telling way she pressed her palms into the counter. 'You have a traitor in your midst.'

Rémy frowned, following Gabe's gaze across the restaurant. 'A…traitor?'

'*Sì.*' Gabe moved across the room, closer to

where she stood. She was trembling slightly now, her expression unmistakably terrified. His own expression remained cool and dismissive, the aloofness he was famed for evident in every line of his hard, muscular frame. No one in that kitchen could have known that beneath his autocratic face and strong body was a pulse that was rushing like a stormy sea.

'What are you talking about?'

'This woman,' Gabe said with quiet determination, 'isn't who you think.' He flicked his gaze from her head to her stomach—which was all he could see of her, owing to the large bench she stood behind. 'She's a liar and a cheat. She's no doubt working here to pick up whatever secrets she can from your customers. If you care at all about your reputation, you'll fire her.'

Rémy moved to stand beside Gabe, his face showing confusion. 'Abby's worked here for over a month.'

'Abby...' Gabe lifted a brow, his expression laced with mockery. It was the name she'd given him too. Far more endearing than Abigail Howard—billion-dollar heiress. 'I think *Abby* is having a laugh at your expense.'

The woman swallowed, the slender column of her throat moving overtime as she sought to moisten her mouth. Gabe caught the betraying gesture with a cynical tilt of his lips.

'That's not true, I swear,' she said, her fingers trembling when she lifted them to her temple and rubbed. Gabe's eyes narrowed. She looked tired. As though she'd been run off her feet all day.

'Oh, you *swear*?' he drawled, moving closer, pressing his palms against the bench. 'You mean we have your *word* that you're telling the truth?'

The words were dripping with sarcasm.

'Please don't do this,' she said softly, with such an appearance of anguish that Gabe could almost have believed her. If he hadn't personally seen what she was capable of.

'Did you know this woman is worth a billion dollars, Rémy? And you've got her, what? Ferrying things from the cold rooms?'

Rémy's surprise was obvious. 'I think you've got the wrong idea about Abby,' he said with a shake of his head, dislodging the pen he kept hooked over one ear.

Gabe's laugh was a short sound of derision. 'I know, better than most, what she's capable of. And, I can tell you, you don't want her anywhere near your patrons.'

'Abby?' Rémy spread his hands wide. 'What's going on?'

She opened her mouth to say something and then shut it again.

Rémy pushed, 'Have you met Mr Arantini before?'

Her eyes flew to Gabe's and, damn it, memories of her straddling him, staring into his eyes as she took him deep within her, spread like wildfire through his blood, burning him from the inside out. He didn't want to remember what she'd been like in his bed. He needed to recall only the way it had ended—with her taking photographs of top secret Calypso documents when she'd believed him to be showering.

His jaw hardened and he leaned forward.

'Tell him how we met, Abigail,' he suggested, and a cold smile iced his lips, almost as though he was enjoying this. He wasn't.

She blinked her eyes closed. 'It doesn't matter,' she muttered under her breath. 'It's ancient history.'

'If only it were,' he said softly. 'But here you are in my friend's kitchen and knowing you, as I do, I can't help but believe you have an ulterior motive.'

'I needed a job,' she said with a shake of her head. 'That's all.'

'Yes, I'm sure you did.' Gabe laughed, but it was a harsh sound, without any true mirth. 'Trust funds are so hard to live off, aren't they?'

'Please—' she focused her energy on Rémy '—I do know this man…' Her eyes shifted to Gabe and her frown deepened. She was an exceptional actress. He could almost have believed she was truly feeling some hint of remorse. Pain. Embarrassment. But he'd been wrong about her once before and he'd never make that mistake again. 'A long time ago. But that's not relevant to why I'm here. I applied for this job because I wanted to work with you. Because I wanted to work. And I'm good at what I do, aren't I?'

Rémy tilted his head. 'Yes,' he conceded. 'But I trust Mr Arantini. We've known one another a long time. If he says I shouldn't have you working here, that I can't trust you…'

Abby froze, disbelief etched across her face. 'You *can* trust me.'

'Like you can trust a starving pit bull at your back door,' Gabe slipped in.

'Monsieur Valiron, I promise you I'm not here for any reason except that I need a job.'

'Needing a job? Another lie,' Gabe said.

'You don't know what you're talking about.' She glared at him and the heat in that look surprised him. The vehemence of her anger. It was as though she were driven to defend herself by something other than pride, by true desperation. He'd felt it often enough to recognise it.

'You forget how well I know what I'm talking about,' he said smoothly. 'You're just lucky I didn't press charges.'

She drew in a shaky breath. 'Mr Arantini,' she said crisply, 'I've moved on from…that…how we met. And you obviously have too.' She blinked her eyes and he had a sinking feeling in his gut that she was trying not to cry.

Hell. He'd never made a woman cry, had he?

Even that night, when he'd accused her, she'd been shocked and devastated, but she hadn't cried. She'd taken his tirade, admitted that her father had asked her to contrive a way to meet him, to get close to him and find out all she could about Calypso, and then she'd apologised. And left.

'I'm not asking you to forgive me for what happened between us.'

'Good,' he interrupted forcibly, wishing now he had a glass of something strong he could drink.

'But please don't ruin this for me.' She turned back to Rémy. 'I'm not lying to you, *monsieur*. I need this job. I have no plans to do anything that will reflect badly on you...'

Rémy frowned. 'I want to believe you, Abby...'

Gabe turned slowly towards his friend, and his expression was cold, unemotional. 'Trusting this woman would be a mistake.'

Abby was numb. It had nothing to do with the snow that was drifting down over New York, turning it into a beautiful winter wonderland, nor the fact she'd left the restaurant in such a hurry she'd forgotten to grab her coat—or her tips.

She swore softly, her head dipped forward, tears running down her cheeks. What were the chances of Gabe Arantini walking into the kitchen of the restaurant she happened to work in? Of his being friendly enough with her boss to actually have her fired?

A sob escaped her and she stopped walking, dipping into an alleyway and pressing herself against the wall for strength.

She'd never thought she'd see him again. She'd tried. She'd tried when she'd thought it mattered. She'd tried when she'd thought it was the right thing to do. But now?

Another sob sounded and she bit down on her lip. He hated her.

She'd always known that, but seeing his cold anger filled her with doubts and fears, making her question what she knew she had to do.

When had he come to New York? Had he been here long? Had he thought of her at all?

She had to see him again—but how? She'd tried calling him so many times, and every call had been unreturned or disconnected. Emails bounced back. She'd even flown to Rome, but he had two burly security men haul her from the building.

So what now?

It would serve that heartless bastard right if she didn't bother. If she skulked off, licking her wounds, keeping her secrets, and doing just what he'd asked: staying the hell away from him.

But it wasn't about what she wanted, nor was it about what Gabe wanted.

She had to think of their baby, Raf—and what he deserved.

Her chest hurt with the pain of the life she was giving their son. Their tiny apartment, their parlous financial state, the fact she worked so hard she barely got to see him, and instead had to have a downstairs neighbour come and stay overnight to help out. It was a mess. And Raf deserved so much better.

For Raf, and Raf alone, Abigail had to find a way to see Gabe—and to tell him the truth.

And this time she wasn't going to let him turn her away without hearing her out first.

CHAPTER TWO

'THERE'S A MISS HOWARD here to see you, sir,' Benita, his assistant, spoke into the intercom.

From the outside Gabe barely reacted, but inside he felt surprise rock him to the core. She'd come to his damned office? What the actual hell? How many times did he have to tell her to stay away from him?

He reached for his phone, lifting it out of the cradle. 'Did you say…?'

'Miss Howard.'

He tightened his grip on the receiver and stared straight ahead. It was a grey day. A gloomy sky stretched over Manhattan, though he knew at street level the city was buzzing with a fever of pre-Christmas activity.

It was on the tip of his tongue to tell his assistant to call the police, when he remembered a small detail. The way Abigail had been two nights earlier, her eyes wet with unshed tears, her lip quivering. As though she really *did* need that menial job.

He knew it to be a lie, of course. But what was the truth? What ruse was she up to? What game was she playing? Was she looking to hurt Rémy? Or was her latest scheme more complex?

He owed it to his friend to find out. But not here.

His office was littered with all manner of documents someone like Abigail would find valuable.

'Tell her I'm busy. She can wait for me, if she'd like,' he said, knowing full well she would wait—and that he'd enjoy stretching that out as long as possible.

He stayed at his desk for the remainder of the day. Hours passed. He caught up on his emails, read the latest report from his warehouse in China, called Noah. It was nearly six when Benita buzzed through.

'I'm all done for the day, Mr Arantini. Unless there's anything else you need?'

'No, Benita.'

'Also, sir, Miss Howard is still here.'

His lips flattened into a grim line. Of course she was.

'Tell her I'm aware she's waiting.'

He disconnected the call and picked up the latest report on Calypso's production, but struggled to focus. Five hours after she'd arrived, the suspense was getting under his skin.

With a heavy sigh, he stood, lifted his jacket from the back of a conference chair and pushed his arms into it, before pulling the door between his office and the reception area open.

It was still well-lit, but the windows behind Abigail were pitch-black. The night sky was heavy and ominous. Despite the fact Christmas was a month away, an enormous tree stood in one corner, and it shone now with the little lights that had been strung through its branches. They cast an almost angelic glow on Abigail. An optical illusion, obviously. There was nothing angelic about this woman.

Her eyes lifted to him at the sound of his entrance, and he ignored the instant spark of attraction that fired in his gut. He was attracted to character traits—intelligence, loyalty, strength of character, integrity. She had none of those things. Well, intelligence, he conceded, but in a way she used for pure evil.

'What do you want?' he asked, deliberately gruff.

She seemed surprised—by his tone? Or the fact he'd actually appeared?

'I didn't think you were going to see me,' she said, confirming that it was the latter. 'I thought you must have already left.'

'My first instinct was to have you removed,' he said. 'You know I'm capable of it.' Now heat stained her cheeks, and her chin tilted defiantly towards him. 'But then it occurred to me that I should find out what you're planning.'

'Planning?'

'Mmm. You must have some reason for working in my friend's kitchen. So? What is it?'

She shook her head. 'Gabe...'

'I prefer you to call me Mr Arantini,' he said darkly. 'It better suits what I think of you and how little I wish to know you.'

She swallowed, and the action drew his attention to the way she'd dressed for this meeting. That was to say, with no particular attempt to impress. Jeans again, though she did wear them well, and a black sweater with a bit of beading around the neckline. She wore ballet slippers on her feet, black as well, but scuffed at the toes.

Her eyes sparked with his, emotions swirling in them. 'Gabe,' she repeated, with a strength he found it difficult not to admire. Not many people could be on the receiving end of Gabe's displeasure and come out fighting. 'The night we met, I was…'

'Stop.' He lifted a hand into the air, his manner imperious. 'I do not want to rehash the past. I don't care about you. I don't care about your father. I don't care about that night except for one reason. You taught me a lesson I'll never forget. I let my guard down with you in a way I hadn't done in years. And you reminded me why I don't make a habit of that.' He said with a shrug that was an emulation of nonchalance, 'Now I want you to get out of my life, for the last time.'

'Listen to me,' she said.

'No!' It was a harsh denial in a silent room. 'Not when every word that comes from your mouth is a self-serving lie.'

She clamped her lips together and his eyes chased the gesture, remembering how her pillowy lower lip had felt between his teeth. A kick of desire flared inside him. Desire? For this woman?

What was wrong with him?

Celibacy, that was what. He should have found someone else for his bed before this—why had he let the ghost of Abby fill his soul for so long?

'You traded your body, your looks, hell, your virginity, because of what it could get you. That makes you no better than...'

He didn't finish the sentence but his implication hung between them, angry and accusing.

'I wanted you, Gabe, just like you wanted me. Calypso wasn't a part of that.' She blinked up at him, and he felt it. The same charge of electricity shot from her to him that had characterised that first night, their first meeting. It was a bolt of lightning; he was rattled by heavy, drugging need. God, would he forgive himself for acting on it? For leaning down and kissing her, for pushing her to the floor and making her his one last time before kicking her out of his life for good?

No.

She had used him; he wouldn't use her.

That wasn't his style. And, no matter how great the sex had been, he sure as hell wasn't going to compromise his own morals just because he happened to find her desirable.

He jerked his gaze away and thrust his hands onto his hips with all the appearance of disregard. 'I don't want you now,' he lied.

'I know that,' she said, a hint of strength in the short words.

'So? What's your plan, Abigail? Why work for Rémy?'

'I need the job—I told you.'

'Yes, yes.' He rolled his eyes. 'You think I'm stupid enough to buy into your lies for a second time?'

She looked startled. 'It's not...it's complicated. And I can't tell you what I came here to say with you glaring at me like you want to strangle me.'

He almost laughed—it was such an insane accusation. 'I don't want to strangle you,' he said. 'I don't want to touch you. I don't want to see you. I'd prefer to think you don't exist.'

She let out a slow, shuddering breath. 'You actually hate me.'

'*Sì.*'

'Okay.' She licked her lower lip. 'I get it. That's...actually strangely good to know.'

'You didn't know this already?'

She shook her head and then changed it to a nod, before pacing slowly across the room. She jammed her hands into her pockets, staring at the shining doors of the lift.

Gabe's impatience grew. He couldn't have said

if it was an impatience to be rid of her or a need to know what the hell she'd come to him to say. Why had he been able to ignore her for a year and now suddenly he was burning up with a desperate need to hear whatever the hell she'd come to him for?

Because he'd seen her again. And he'd felt that same tug of powerful attraction, that was why. He needed to exercise caution—it was a slippery slope with Abigail, almost as though she were a witch, imbued with magical powers to control and contort him. There was danger in her proximity. The sooner he could be free of her, the better.

'So?' he demanded when she didn't speak. 'What's going on? Why are you here? What do you want this time?'

She was wary. 'Well, I'd like my job back,' she said, somewhat sarcastically.

'Pigs might fly,' he said. 'You're just lucky I didn't tell Rémy the full sordid story of how we met.'

'Would it have mattered? He fired me anyway.' She narrowed her eyes. 'Did that give you satisfaction? To see me embarrassed like that? To see me thrown out?'

He considered it for a moment, his expression hard. 'Yes.'

She squeezed her eyes shut and tilted her head

towards the ceiling, breathing in, steadying herself. 'You're a bastard.'

'So I've been told.'

He looked down at her again. She was slim. Too slim. Her figure had been pleasingly rounded when they'd met, curves in all the places Gabe—and any red-blooded man—fantasised about. Now, she was supermodel slender.

Her body was a minefield of distraction, but he'd been down that path before. No good would come from worshipping her physical perfection. He refocused his attention on the matter at hand: the sooner they dealt with it, the sooner she'd be gone and this would be over.

'Why does it matter?' he demanded. 'We both know you don't need to work—even if poor Rémy was foolish enough to believe your act. So, what's the big deal?'

'You're wrong.'

'Rarely.'

'I needed that job. I needed the money.'

'Your father's company?' he asked, frowning, a hint of something like genuine interest colouring the words. 'It hasn't gone bankrupt?' He'd have heard, surely.

'No—' she shook her head '—I think he's holding it together. But I don't know. I haven't spoken to him in a long time.'

'Oh?' Gabe was no longer losing interest in this.

His blood was racing through his body and he took a step towards her, unconsciously moving closer. 'Why is that?'

She swallowed, and appeared to be weighing her words—something Gabe hated. Liars always thought about what they wanted to say, and she was an exceptional liar.

'He threw me out,' she said, the words tremulous even though her eyes met his with a fierce strength.

'He...threw you out?' Gabe, rarely surprised, felt that emotion now. 'Your father?'

'Yes.'

Why was he so shocked? He knew enough of cruel fathers and their ability to abuse their children's affections to know Lionel Howard was capable of everything Abigail claimed.

'Because of me?'

She nodded.

Gabe's curse was softly voiced but forceful, and it filled the room. 'Your father threw you out because you didn't have photos of the Calypso project?'

'No.' She shook her head, her skin pale. 'Not exactly.'

Gabe waited, but his impatience was making it difficult.

'I mean, he was furious that morning. Furious that I had come back empty-handed. But it was a fury born of desperation, you know? He was desperate, Gabe. My dad isn't a bad person, he's just...'

'Why,' he interrupted coldly, 'do you think I want to talk about your father?'

'You have to understand...'

She was quicksand. He'd let her in and now he was sinking—back into her web of lies, her intriguing fascination. What a fool he'd been to think he could talk to her and not fall down this rabbit hole of desire.

'No, I don't. I don't "have" to do anything where you're concerned. I don't know why you're here. I don't know why I didn't have you escorted from the building. But I'm done. This is over.'

'Wait.' She licked her lower lip and then lifted her hand to her hair, toying with the ends in an unmistakably nervous gesture. 'I'm trying to explain.'

'Explain what?'

'That night—it wasn't what you think. I mean, I know I came to you because of Calypso, but from the minute I met you, that was just about you and me, and the way we felt.'

'And yet you still took photographs. You thought you could have your cake and eat it too? A night with me *and* the chance to salvage your father's company thrown into the mix?'

'No. I didn't think it through, obviously.' She

pulled a face. 'I know it's no excuse and it must sound pathetic to someone like you. It's just... I've always done what he asked of me. It's hard to rewire that.'

'He asked you to do something borderline illegal.'

'I know!' she growled—a growl born of self-disgust. 'I wish, again and again, I could undo that night.' Her cheeks flushed. 'I mean, not *all* of it.'

'Ah,' he said with dangerous softness. 'Here we differ. Because if I had my way I would go back in time and *never* meet you. Never set eyes on you, never kiss you, never ask you to my room. I would undo every little bit of what we shared. I regret *everything* about knowing you.'

Her mouth dropped open. He'd hurt her. He'd shocked her. Good. He recognised, in the part of his brain that was still working properly, that he liked that. He liked seeing that pain on her face. She deserved it. It was only a hint of how he'd felt when he'd discovered that his lover was actually some kind of corporate spy.

'And now,' he said, 'if you'll excuse me, I have a date.'

Yes. He'd definitely landed that blow successfully. She physically reeled, spinning away from him in a poor attempt to conceal her reaction.

'When I told Dad I hadn't met you, he was angry. Angry because he'd told me exactly where you'd be. Angry because he thought I hadn't tried hard enough.'

'Yet you're an accomplished liar,' Gabe pointed out. 'So I'm sure you managed to win him over.'

She didn't react. Her eyes were glazed over, as though she were in the past. 'Not really. I mean, he stopped being mad with me, but his business worries grew. He was losing his market share to you; he has been for years—'

'It's not *his* market share. It's anyone's for the taking. And the only reason Bright Spark is at the top of the ladder is because we release better products than our competitors.'

'I know.' She nodded, almost apologetically. 'I'm just explaining his mindset.'

'Whatever his mindset, you are your own person. You made a decision to manipulate me…'

'I'm talking about after that,' she said with quiet determination. 'You know I've been trying to contact you.'

He tilted his head. 'Apologies are fruitless, Abigail. There is no apology you could offer that would inspire my forgiveness. You're a liar and a cheat.'

She shook her head but didn't say anything. 'It was bad at home. I was worried about him, and I didn't feel well.'

Gabe lifted his brows.

'When did you not feel well?'

'A few months after we…after that night. I'd been tired—yet not sleeping.'

'Guilt will do that to a person. Then again, I don't know if you're capable of feeling guilt.'

'Believe me, I am,' she promised, the words steady, so that he was at risk of believing her despite everything he knew her to be. 'I've felt a bucketload of it since I met you. Anyway, I went to the doctor and…you can probably guess where I'm going with this.'

'No,' he said with a lift of his shoulders. 'And frankly I'm bored of our conversation.'

'Right, you have your date,' she said, the words almost manic.

'Yes,' Gabe lied. Well, not strictly a lie. There were any number of women he could call. Just because he hadn't done so in over a year didn't mean they wouldn't jump at the chance for a night with Gabe Arantini. He stared at Abigail for one long moment and then made to walk past her, only she reached out and grabbed his arm. 'Gabe, stop. You need to let me say this.'

'Why do you think I owe you anything?'

'I was pregnant,' she said, arresting him in his tracks completely. His eyes locked onto hers and in his face was a torrent of emotions. There was anger, disbelief, confusion, fury and, finally, amusement.

'Nice try, Abigail, but I don't believe you. You

think this is a way to extort money from me? Or ruin me somehow? Is this your father's idea?'

'No!' She was pale and shaking. 'Gabe, I'm not making this up. I went to the doctor and they ran some tests. I was pregnant. You're the only man I've ever been with.'

His eyes narrowed.

'I didn't tell Dad until I was five months along and I started to show. He demanded to know who the father was and when I told him he...'

Gabe could barely keep up, but somehow he answered calmly. 'Yes?'

'He kicked me out. He cut me off. I haven't seen him since.'

Gabe felt as though he'd been punched in the solar plexus. He couldn't speak.

'It's why I need that job. Why I'm working nights. I have a good babysitter who sleeps over, so I can work at night. And in the days I'm with Raf.'

His eyes flew wide. 'Raf?'

'Rafael,' she said with a small, distracted smile. 'Our son.'

Silence fell, heavy and caustic, in the room. Gabe processed what she'd said, but it simply didn't make sense.

'We used protection.'

'I know.'

'It's not possible.'

'The three-month-old I have at home would beg to differ,' she said calmly, even when her nerves were jangling.

Gabe nodded, a coldness to his expression. 'What is this? You want money? Or something else?'

'I thought you should know,' she said with hauteur, reminding him of the silver spoon she'd grown up with.

'You thought I should know that I'm a father. That supposedly the night we were together, you fell pregnant. How convenient!'

'Not particularly,' Abby said with a soft laugh.

'Do you think I am this stupid? That I'll listen to these lies? I should have followed my first instincts and had you kicked out. What the hell are you playing at?'

'It's the *truth*,' she said. 'I have a son. His name is Raf Arantini and he's the spitting image of his father.'

Gabe glared at her. She'd even used his name? Could it be true?

Presumably she hadn't been on birth control, but he never slept with a woman without protection. And he'd never had any consequences come from his sex life before. So why now? And why this woman?

Because she was a liar. And though he couldn't see the full picture, he knew with confidence that there was more to this story than she was telling him. It *couldn't* be the truth. There was no way on earth he had a baby.

He needed time and space to think, and he sure as hell couldn't do that with her in the room.

'Get out of my office, Abigail. And don't contact me again.'

He walked to the lift and pressed the button; it pinged open almost instantly.

She walked slowly and as she passed him he caught just a hint of her sweet vanilla fragrance. His whole body clenched.

'You don't believe me?' she asked.

'Do you blame me?'

Tears welled in her eyes but she met his eyes with obvious defiance. 'It's the truth.'

'I don't think you'd know the truth if it bit you on that perfect little arse of yours.'

CHAPTER THREE

ABIGAIL STARED OUT of the window, unseeing. It was a cold, snowy night, but she hadn't put the heating on. Raf was bundled up in a fleecy suit and wrapped in blankets, fast asleep, and she was wearing about six layers. She wrapped her hands around her hot chocolate—it was a pale imitation, seeing as she'd taken to making it with water instead of milk, but it was still sweet and warm—desperately necessary after the day she'd had.

She'd gone over her conversation with Gabe all evening—while he was no doubt out at some glamorous restaurant or bar with an equally glamorous woman. He probably wasn't even giving her a second thought. Why would he be? He'd made it clear he despised her and, more importantly, didn't believe her. So why would he be thinking about a baby he didn't believe existed?

She should have shown him a photograph, but Abigail hadn't been thinking straight. A photograph would have convinced him of his paternity. They were so alike—Raf had Gabe's dark eyes, his strong determined brow and curling black hair, though the dimples in his cheeks were all Abby's. She curled up in the armchair by the window and watched as a child dressed as an elf ran past, followed by a happy-looking mum and dad, also wearing elf hats.

Fliers had been up in the street for weeks—tonight was one of the local school's Christmas concerts—which explained why there'd been a procession of Wise Men and reindeer shuffling around her Brooklyn neighbourhood since she'd returned.

While Abigail hadn't expected Gabe to be doing cartwheels about the fact he was a father, nor had she expected his reaction—utter disbelief.

For months, she'd tried to find a way to tell him about the baby they'd conceived. First, when she'd been pregnant, and then once Raf had been born. It had never, not for an instant, occurred to her that he wouldn't believe her. She had run through almost every contingency—but not this one.

The coldness of his expression as she'd stepped into the lift and turned back to face him would always be etched into her mind. He *hated* her. He'd said as much, and in that moment she knew it to be true.

So, what was she going to do?

She looked around the apartment, empty save for a threadbare chair, a plastic table, a lamp that she'd bought at a thrift shop, and she felt hopelessness well inside her.

Even with her job, she'd barely been making ends meet. Now? She had forty-seven dollars in her bank account, rent was due and her baby needed formula and nappies. Before long, he'd need actual food and bigger clothes, and then what?

She couldn't keep living like this. Raf deserved so much better.

She finished the hot chocolate and placed the empty cup on the floor at her feet and then curled her legs up beneath her.

Exhaustion was nothing new to Abigail. Pregnancy had been exhausting and she'd been sick almost the whole time. But then Raf had been born and she'd discovered that motherhood was a little like being hit by a truck. She was bone-weary all the time.

Her eyes were heavy and she was so tired that even the thought of getting up, showering and changing for bed seemed too onerous and so she stayed where she was, telling herself she'd just sleep for a moment. Just a little rest. Then she'd go to bed, wake up in the new day and scour the papers for help wanted ads. She'd get a new job. Gabe couldn't have her fired from every place in the city.

A knock at the door woke her after drifting off. It was persistent and loud—so loud she was certain it would wake Raf if she didn't act quickly. She scrambled up and moved towards the door, yanking it inwards without taking the precaution of checking who was there—a foolish risk given that the downstairs security door had been busted for weeks.

Still, she had thought it might be the upstairs neighbour, Mrs Hannigan, who seemed to always need something at inconvenient times. Even this though—nearly midnight—was a stretch for her.

Abby hadn't expected—foolishly, perhaps—to find Gabe Arantini on her doorstep, his handsome face lined with emotions she couldn't comprehend.

'Gabe?' The word was thick with sleepiness. She ran the back of her hand over her eyes in an attempt to wake up, but it only induced a yawn. 'What are you doing here? How did you find where I live?'

His response was to brush past her and step into her apartment.

'By all means, come right in,' she snapped sarcastically. But the tart emotion disappeared almost as soon as it had arrived, swallowed by a sense of self-consciousness for him to be seeing her threadbare apartment.

'Where is he?'

'I… He's sleeping.'

'Of course he is,' he said, the same thread of incredulity in his words now as had been there earlier that day.

He still didn't believe her? How was that possible? She would just show him a photo. Her phone was on the chair. She'd get it and show some pictures to him. Then he'd have no doubt that she was telling the truth. She moved in that direction but his voice stilled her.

'Stop, Abigail.'

She froze, turning around to face him once more. He was right behind her, his body close to hers, his angular face filling her vision.

'No more lies.'

'I'm not lying to you.'

He lifted a finger and pressed it to her lips. 'I think you don't even realise you're doing it,' he said. 'I think you've lost sight of what's true and what's not.'

'I…'

'Shh…' he said again, shaking his head. 'I didn't come here to hear more lies…'

'Then why…?'

His eyes held hers and Abigail grabbed a deep breath because she knew what was coming and she had about two seconds to decide what she would do. Step backwards, away from him, or surrender to the intimacy of his kiss, even knowing it was stupid and wrong and wouldn't achieve anything?

But oh, how she craved him. Ached for him. Desperately longed for him.

He was going to kiss her and she was going to let him. Heck, *she* was going to kiss *him* if he took much longer. The air around them seemed to hum and crackle with anticipation, their eyes locked, their lips parted. Time seemed to stand still. It was madness, but hadn't it always been for them?

He dropped his head infinitesimally closer and she pressed a little higher, waiting, her mind blanked of the myriad reasons she shouldn't let this happen.

Then he blinked and straightened.

'What the hell is that?'

The question jolted her, dragging her out of the sensual fog.

'Raf!' She shot him a look of frustration and sanity began to seep back in. Gratitude too. How could she have let herself get sucked back into his sensual, distracting appeal?

In the seconds it took her to compute the situation, Gabe was already moving to the hallway. There was a bathroom on one side and a bedroom on the other. He followed the sound of the crying and pushed into the bedroom. He stood just inside the door, staring at the crib as though he'd never seen a baby in his entire life.

'Excuse me,' Abby said, moving past him to scoop up Raf. He nuzzled into her and she stroked his head, her eyes lifting to Gabe's with a hint of triumph in their depths.

'What is this?' he finally asked, dumbfounded.

'What do you think?'

'It's a baby.'

She could have laughed; it was so absurd. 'Yes, it's a baby. This is your son. You may remember I told you about him this afternoon?'

'I…' Gabe stared at the child with a look of utter confusion.

'He needs to go back to sleep,' she said, nodding towards the door. And purely because he was at such a loss he did as she suggested and stepped out of the room, leaving her to settle Raf on her own.

When Abby emerged a few moments later, Gabe was in the centre of the tiny living room, his expression grim.

'You were telling the truth.'

'Yes!' she said emphatically. 'Why would you think I wasn't?'

He frowned. 'You need to ask that?'

'Gabe, I made a mistake that night. Admittedly, a big one. I get why you're mad. But it was a *mistake*. A stupid decision. Contrary to what you might think, I don't make a habit of lying to people.'

He rubbed his palm over his face and shook his head. 'How is this even possible?'

'Really? You need me to explain how that works?'

'I mean, we used protection.'

'Yeah. The doctor said that's not infallible.'

He grimaced. 'It was your first time. This shouldn't have been possible.'

'Okay, you need to stop saying that. You're the only man I've ever been with and nine months after that night, almost to the day, Raf was born. So, whether it should or shouldn't have been possible, that's what happened.'

'You should have told me,' he said, harsh judgement in the statement.

Abby made a primal noise of irritation, a growl born of pure annoyance. She would be the first to admit she'd messed up the night they'd met, but she wasn't going to be tarred with that brush for evermore. 'I tried to! Damn it, Gabe, why did you think I was calling you?'

He paled visibly beneath his tan. 'You… I presumed to apologise, or make up excuses.'

'No. I mean yes to the apology thing, but mainly, Gabe, I needed to tell you about Raf.'

'You're saying you didn't keep him from me intentionally?'

'Are you serious? Do you really think I'd do something so immoral?'

His eyes locked onto hers and she sighed.

'I guess you do think me capable of that. But Gabe, I would never, ever keep someone from their child. He's your son. I had no intention of doing this alone. That's why I went to Rome…'

'Rome.' His eyes swept shut, anguish on his features. 'You knew you were pregnant then? You came to tell me?'

'Yes!' Pique at his reaction darkened her expression. 'And you had me dragged out like some kind of criminal.'

'*Madre di Dio*, Abigail. I didn't know.'

'Yes, well,' she said stiffly. 'If you'd given me a minute of your time, you'd have seen for yourself the evidence of my condition.'

'What do you mean?'

'I was six months along.'

'And they just dragged you out of the building?'

'Well, they told me in no uncertain terms to go before the police arrived,' she conceded.

'I asked them to do that,' he admitted darkly. 'I didn't want to see you. I was so angry you'd come.'

'I know.' She lifted her chin, defiance radiating from her slender frame. 'But don't you dare accuse me of intentionally keeping Raf from you.'

He shook his head, as if to clear the memory. 'I cannot believe I have a son.'

What could Abby say to that? It was the truth. She waited for something—perhaps an apology. A commendation of how well she'd done? An admission that she'd *tried* to do the right thing, to tell him the truth?

And got instead: 'And you're raising him here? Like this?'

Her spine straightened and she squared her shoulders. 'What's wrong with it?' she said.

'It is a hovel.' He glared at her. 'How can you live like this?'

Her jaw dropped. His assessment wasn't wrong but how dare he?

'It's fine,' she said through gritted teeth. 'And I'll find something better before he's big enough to notice. For *now*, this is fine,' she amended.

'This isn't *fine* for a pack of rabid dogs, let alone my *son*.'

She stared at him as though he'd called her the worst name in the book. 'I'm aware that it's not ideal. I'm not blind. But it's the best I could do at short notice and with very limited means.'

A muscle in his jaw throbbed and Abby stared at it, fascinated by the pulse point there. 'So when your father discovered you were pregnant with my child, he turned you out of his home?'

She winced. 'It was more complex than that. I mean, it proved that I'd lied about that night. That I'd let him down.'

'Let him down?' Gabe repeated incredulously. '*Dio!* He is unbelievable.'

'I know that,' she said. 'I never thought he'd react like this. I mean, I thought he'd be angry, but not…'

'To remove all financial support from his pregnant daughter, just because he hates me?' Something in Gabe shifted and he was very still, his expression faraway, as though completely consumed by unpleasant thoughts.

Abby waited, her breath unconsciously held, for him to elaborate.

But in the end he shook his head. 'It doesn't matter. You are no longer his responsibility.'

'I'm no one's responsibility,' she said stiffly, instantly rejecting that assessment.

'Wrong, *cara*. You are mine.'

'No.' Abby's denial was swift.

'You are the mother of my child.'

Her hackles rose. 'I'm a woman you spent one night with, a year ago.'

'*Sì*. And you fell pregnant. I should have prevented that. I was experienced. This is my fault.'

'Your fault?' Now her maternal instincts roared to life. 'I don't consider Raf anyone's *fault*. He's a blessing.'

Gabe grimaced, uncharacteristically on the back foot. 'I didn't mean that the way it sounded.'

But she wasn't to be placated. She had to set the record straight while she had a chance—if she didn't control this, the situation could quickly move beyond her control. 'You don't owe me anything, Gabe. I'm not asking for a handout.'

'You live like *this*,' he said slowly, gesturing around the room, 'and you think I don't owe you anything?'

Frustration burst through her. 'I know this place isn't...'

'It's a dump.'

The insult hurt. 'It's home, for now.'

He crossed his arms over his chest, his expression intractable.

'You say you wanted to tell me about the baby?'

She nodded.

'And what did you expect me to say?'

Abby frowned, but her silence only seemed to spur him on. He took a step closer, his expression grim.

'What did you want from me?'

She swallowed, and tried to find the words of the speech she'd imagined she'd give him, if ever he learned the truth. 'Raf is your child too, and I respect the fact you might want to be involved in his upbringing.'

'Oh, yes?' he murmured, but there was a sharpness to the response, an underlying firmness she didn't understand.

'Your life is in Italy and we live here, but I mean, you visit the States and I guess, when he's older, he could come over...'

Her sentence tapered off into silence. His eyes held hers for a long, icy moment. Then, with a guttural sound of disgust, 'Look at this place, Abigail!' He glared at her. 'Why is it so cold? Why is the heating off?' He stalked into the kitchenette and ripped open the fridge. 'What are you existing on? I see two apples and one bread roll. What did you have for dinner?'

She bit down on her lip and ridiculous tears moistened her eyes. She dashed at them angrily. 'I'm not crying because I'm sad,' she clarified. 'I'm mad! And I'm tired! And you have no right turning up on my doorstep at midnight only to throw insults at my feet!'

'What did you think I would do? How am I supposed to react?'

'I…' She glared at him. 'I don't know. I just had to tell you.'

He dipped his head forward in silent concession. 'I'm grateful that you did. And for the fact you haven't used our son to attempt to blackmail me.'

'Blackmail you?' she repeated, aghast, flicking her fair hair over one shoulder. 'What would I blackmail you for?'

His laugh was short and sharp. 'Oh, I don't know. Money. Power. Calypso prototypes?'

Abby had never hit a man in her life—or anyone, for that matter, but her fingertips itched to strike his arrogant face. 'You're a jerk.'

'I'm the father of your child and, like it or not, I'm in your life now.'

She was very still, waiting for that thought to make sense. But it didn't. 'In my life how?'

Gabe shut the fridge door and moved to the pantry. It was almost empty, save for a tin of spaghetti and a bag of pasta.

'How quickly can you pack a suitcase?'

'Huh?' She watched as he stalked back into the small living room.

'Your wardrobe looked small. I presume you don't have much. Is there a bag somewhere?'

'I… No.' She'd sold her designer set of luggage as soon as she'd moved into the apartment.

'Fine. I'll have one sent over.'

'Gabe, wait.' She lifted a hand in a determined appeal for his silence. 'I don't need a suitcase. I'm not going anywhere.'

He ignored her, speaking as though she hadn't. 'It's too late to depart now. You should go to bed. I'll…take the chair. We can leave in the morning.'

'And where exactly do you imagine we're going?'

'Italy.' He reached for his phone and, before she could respond, he began speaking into it. She had not a hope of comprehending as he spoke in his native tongue, but she picked out a few words— *bambino…andiamo…subito.*

He disconnected the call before giving Abby the full force of his attention.

'The plane will be ready in the morning. My car is downstairs. Tomorrow, Abigail, we will leave.'

She shook her head emphatically. 'No!'

'Yes.'

'I'm not going to Italy. This is my home. *His* home. And you... I know you're his father, but I didn't tell you so you'd take us away! I just wanted you to know because he's your child and at some stage he or you might want a relationship. I don't believe in secrets like this, okay? I have no right to keep a father from his child. But that's the end of it. I've done my part. I told you about Raf, and when he's older I'll tell him about you.'

His eyes narrowed and his chest lifted with the force of the deep breath he sucked in. 'Get ready. This is non-negotiable.'

'You're right. It's non-negotiable. We're staying here.'

'Make no mistake about it, Abigail, my son is coming to Italy. I am giving you a chance to come with him. The decision is yours.'

Panic flared in her gut but she hid it behind anger. 'There's no way you can do that.'

'Do you want to test that theory?'

'You seriously think I'm going to move to a foreign country with a man I hardly know?'

'No. I think you're going to move to a foreign country with the man you're going to marry.'

Her eyes flew wide and for a moment she thought she must have misheard. 'What did you just say?'

His jaw tightened. 'You heard me.'

'But that's crazy.'

He jerked his head in silent agreement.

She blinked. 'But why?'

Something like anguish shifted through his dark gaze, showing how clearly he wished this step weren't necessary. 'Because it's the right thing to do.'

'Right, how?' she demanded, wondering if she'd slipped through the looking glass into a bizarre parallel universe.

'Because of what I can offer him, and what I can offer you. The security, the comfort, the support.' He took a step closer. 'I'm offering you the world, Abigail. The world for you and our son.'

Her heart twisted painfully inside her chest. She was like an outsider looking in. In that moment, she realised that marrying Gabe Arantini would have, in another lifetime, constituted a fantasy. If things had been different between them, if they'd met under different circumstances and they'd been allowed to enjoy getting to know one another.

'This is the twenty-first century. People don't get married just because of a baby.'

His eyes narrowed and she had the strangest sense that he was holding back on saying what he really wanted to say. Through teeth that were bared like a wolf's, he said, 'My son is going to grow up with two parents.'

'Who hate each other? Do you really think that's best?'

'No.' His eyes glowed with silent warning. 'But it's the best decision you can make. I have a son, Abigail. A three-month-old boy I knew nothing about. If you think I am leaving this country without him, if you think I have any plans of walking out of his life, even temporarily, then you are deranged.'

She sucked in a breath but her lungs didn't fill sufficiently. She dug her fingernails into her palms, taking strength from the gesture. 'Then stay here,' she said after a moment, the words sounding reasonable and calm despite the tremors taking over her central nervous system.

He looked around the room with scathing contempt.

'Not *here* here,' she amended. 'In New York.'

His eyes locked onto hers. 'I have no intention of raising my child anywhere other than Italy. We will go there tomorrow and as soon as possible we will marry. Raf will grow up believing that he is wanted.'

'He is wanted by me!' she shouted and then winced at the very real possibility that such loud arguing would wake their son.

'And by me,' he said warningly.

'No. I think it's time for you to leave, Gabe. We can discuss this in the morning when you're thinking straight.'

'Do you think you have any right to dictate to me after what you've done?'

'What I've done?' she demanded, taking a step closer, wishing she were taller so that she didn't have to crane her neck to look up at him. 'And just what am I supposed to have done?'

'You set all this in motion when you came to my hotel last year. Even if there had been no baby, no Raf, you have still shown yourself capable of making very poor decisions.'

'You got that right,' Abby muttered. 'Sleeping with you was the biggest mistake of my life.'

She swept her eyes shut, instantly wishing she could retract the words because of course she could never really regret anything that had resulted in Raf. Besides, even without Raf, she'd be hard-pressed to regret what she and Gabe had shared. Only that her father's machinations had been the cause of it.

'I feel exactly the same way.' The coolly delivered response slammed right into her heart and suddenly all the emotions of the previous year filled her up, like water in a bathtub.

'Oh, go to hell,' she muttered, slumping back against the wall and dipping her head forward.

'I think I'm already there.'

The volley landed squarely in her chest, twisting her organs and supercharging her blood. She swallowed, but her throat was drier than the desert.

Two days ago she'd been working as a kitchen hand for one of New York's most renowned chefs. She'd been exhausted and lonely but she'd been making it work.

And now she had this man, this handsome, arrogant billionaire who she couldn't be in the same room as without breaking into a full-blown fight, demanding that she move halfway around the world and become his wife? Mrs Gabe Arantini?

She couldn't marry him! God, what a nightmare! Why had she ever thought she had to tell him about his son? At least without seeing a lawyer first! Why had she been so naive? She should have kept Raf hidden from him. She should have moved heaven and earth to avoid this.

What an idiot she was!

'I won't marry you,' she said angrily, her blood simmering. 'I can't. It would never work.'

'Believe me, the last thing I *want* is to legally bind myself to you—or your father, for that matter.' His eyes glazed with determination. 'But it is the only way this will work. These are my terms, *tempesta*.'

'It makes no sense.' The words were stoic when her chest was crushing under the weight of his demands.

He stared at her long and hard. 'I told you, I

want our son to have a family. That's…very important to me.' The words were spoken with an iron-like determination but, even without that, Abby found the concept dug deep into her chest. A family? What would that be like? It had been so long since her mother had died, she could barely remember a time when they'd been a collective. Her father had emotionally shut her out many long years before he'd finally cut their ties altogether.

Abby was alone in the world. Her beloved mother was dead, her father had slammed the door on her, and now Gabe was threatening to take Raf away. She couldn't lose her son; she wouldn't let her son lose her either!

But, far from losing him, what if she could give him exactly what Gabe was offering? What if she could give Raf a real family?

'A marriage born of hate cannot work,' she said dubiously, her eyes flicking to his before skimming away.

He spoke softly, considering each word. 'There is love too. I saw my son and loved him instantly. You are his mother. That means something to me, Abigail. No matter how I feel about you personally, I wish you no ill. I want to take care of you as well. Raf deserves that—to know that his father will protect his mother.' Deep emotions rang through that last sentence, as though he'd dredged it up from deep within his soul.

She wanted to fight him. She wanted to tell him that what she most needed protection from was the power Gabe wielded over her, and the ease with which he could hurt her. She wanted to shout at him and rail against him but the last year had been long and draining for Abigail, and all the pluck she'd once held in her armoury had been dulled to the point of non-existence. Her fight had been washed away; sleeplessness and loneliness, abandonment and discord with her father had made her heart sore and heavy. She wanted to fight Gabe, she wanted to fight him so badly, but every day had been a battle and she found—in that moment—she had very little fight left.

What he offered was so tempting. She swept her eyes shut, desperately trying to rally some strength, some fight, some determination to keep him at a distance.

'I don't know how it would work.'

'We don't need to discuss semantics now.'

'It's not semantics!' she insisted, reaching out a hand and wrapping her fingers around his wrist. 'This is my life. Mine and Raf's. You can't expect me to just *marry* you.'

He expelled a sigh, a sound of impatience. 'Why not?'

'Seriously? Why not? I could give you a thousand reasons.'

'I'm not interested in a thousand. Give me a single good one.'

His manner was imposing at the best of times but now, in this conversation, she could barely scrape her thoughts together.

She clutched at the first straw she found. 'I hardly know you.'

'How is that relevant?' he said with a shake of his head.

'You're asking me to move to Italy and become your wife…'

'I'm suggesting you choose the best-case scenario in this *situation*.' He stared at her resolutely. 'It is, of course, your decision.'

Her heart sank.

Her decision?

She was broke, alone, and hardly ever saw her tiny baby because of the hours she had to work just to get by. Everything she did was for Raf; wouldn't she hurt her son by denying him all that Gabe could offer?

She was terrified of the way this man made her feel, but wasn't motherhood about putting your child's needs above your own? All she had to do, in order to make this decision, was ignore her own needs and wants and think of what was best for Raf.

Then the decision was a simple one.

She wanted Raf to have the best life in the

world—she wanted to give that to him. She just had to dance with the devil…

Living with Gabe wouldn't be a walk in the park, and nor would marriage to him. But for Raf? What wouldn't she do? With a look of fierce strength and resolve, she nodded. 'Fine. You win. We'll come to Italy.'

'You'll marry me.' It wasn't a question, but he clearly wanted her to answer.

'On one condition.'

He arched a brow, but said nothing.

Abby hadn't been sure what she wanted to say, only that she knew she had to demand something of him—anything—to assert her position as an intelligent woman. Yielding power to him would be a disaster. 'If I move to Italy and marry you—'

'When,' he interrupted, his expression daring her to disagree.

'When I marry you,' she agreed with soft defiance, 'you'll be a good father to him. You'll spend time with him. He's not a trophy son to be loved on Christmases and birthdays. I'm only doing this for Raf, so he'll have what I…'

The sentence tapered off, a sense of betrayal forestalling her from adding: *what I never had.*

But Gabe knew. He understood what kind of father she'd had, or rather hadn't.

'I will be a hands-on father, Abigail. You can rest assured on that score.'

She expelled a soft breath. He *would* be a good father; she had no doubts. He might hate her, and perhaps with good reason, but she could see how much he wanted this, how much he already loved their son.

'Fine,' she said, holding his gaze even when she wanted to squeeze her eyes shut and blot out reality for a little longer.

There was a brief glimmer of triumph in the coal-dark depths of his eyes, but then he nodded. 'We'll leave in the morning.'

CHAPTER FOUR

'WHERE ARE WE going to, Mamma?' Gabe asked, his six-year-old self huddled beside Marina's slim frame.

'On an adventure, darling. Far from here. To a happy place, full of sunshine and oceans and friendly people.'

'Sunshine *all the time*?'

'Yes, Gabe. Somewhere life will be kind, where you will be happy, and me too.' She crouched down, her eyes meeting his. 'And your father.'

'Papà?'

'*Sì.*'

'He's going to come with us?'

'He'll visit.' She smiled mysteriously. He didn't see Marina smile often. It was nice. He was glad.

'I'll get to meet my father?'

'You will.' She reached into her pocket and pulled out a sweet. 'He gave me this, for you. For the flight.'

'We're going on an aeroplane?'

'Oh, yes, Gabe. Australia is far away, across many oceans. It will take a long time to get there, but it's worth it.'

'How do you know?'

'Because when I was a little girl, I lived there,

and I loved it. And because your father says so, *dolci*, and he's never wrong. He's going to take care of us from now on. No more struggling, no more worries. Just sunshine and happiness for you and me.' She kissed his head and ruffled his hair, and then smiled in a way he hadn't known her capable of. 'Pack your bag, little love. It's time to go.'

He slept in the lounge. Abby hadn't expected that, but at one point during the night, having tossed and turned for hours, she got up to get a glass of water and saw Gabe's broad sleeping frame huddled in the dilapidated recliner nearest to the window. It was a tatty chair, but it was her favourite spot to curl up in and read a book.

The sight of his body crumpled into it arrested her in her tracks. She froze, just inside the kitchenette, her eyes hungrily devouring every single detail in a way she'd never have allowed herself to do were he awake.

He'd stripped off his suit jacket and discarded it over the back of another chair, and his tie too. His shirt was unbuttoned at the neck, revealing the strong, thick column of his neck, and his sleeves were pushed up to reveal tanned forearms.

He breathed deeply, his broad chest lifting with each inhalation.

In the year since they'd been together, she'd dreamed of him often. But they were never coherent dreams, nor were they sensible. They were fractured memories. His body over hers, their eyes locked, fingers entwined, lips meshing. Their breathing in unison, laughing, his voice as he whispered Italian words into her ears, words that she couldn't understand but became addicted to hearing.

The way he'd held her tight as he'd pushed past her innocence, reassuring her with his words and his body that she would be all right. That he would keep her safe.

She swallowed and took a step closer to him without realising it. He shifted in the chair and she froze, swallowing guiltily, heat spreading through her cheeks.

He was a beautiful specimen of masculinity. When she'd met him, she'd been rendered speechless by the strength and power that emanated from him. There was confidence and control in every breath he issued. He was inherently remarkable. But now, in repose, there was something even more fascinating, even more appealing.

There was a raw vulnerability in his face as he slept, almost as if she could peel back the layers of time and see Gabe as he'd been years earlier, as a child. Had he always been confident in a way that bordered on arrogance? Had he been feted and worshipped in those early years of his life, so that the seeds of self-belief had been firmly planted in the make-up of his soul? Or had he become like this later? In his teens? Twenties? Had something happened that had shaped him, such as his phenomenal success?

Abigail discounted it instantly. He and his business partner were self-made success stories. To achieve what they had took a huge amount of confidence, as well as intelligence and ability. Success hadn't shaped him—he'd reached for success with both hands. That determination and grit was fundamentally Gabe.

'You're staring.'

She was startled, her eyes flying back to his face, heat intensifying in her cheeks as she realised he was awake, languidly watching her—watching her watch him. Embarrassment curdled her blood.

'I...thought you might be cold,' she lied huskily. 'Do you need a blanket?'

His lips curled derisively, showing he understood exactly why she'd been staring at him.

'I'm warm enough.' There was a mocking challenge in his expression.

'Good.' She swallowed.

'You cannot sleep?' he prompted after a moment.

She shook her head. 'My mind can't stop spinning. I can't stop thinking about the madness of what I've agreed to.'

He made a soft noise. 'There's no point thinking about what is already done.'

'It's not done, though,' she said with a shrug.

'Are you trying to tell me you've changed your mind?'

Was she? She stared at him, her heart still thundering through her body like a runaway horse in a storm. She bit down on her lip and closed her eyes, trying to sift through her wants and needs, her certainties and doubts.

'Raf deserves what you can give him,' she said finally, with a shake of her head. 'I know that.'

'I'm going to take care of you both, Abigail.' The words held a strange other-worldly quality. 'You will have nothing to worry about from now on. *Capisce?*'

She carried his assurance to bed, strangely warmed by it when she had no real reason to trust him.

The next morning broke over New York cold and bleak.

'Are you packed?' Gabe was waiting when Abby stepped out of the bathroom.

She stared at him, her heart jolting at this version of Gabe. All arrogant, in-control tycoon once more, dressed in his suit, his dark hair pushed back from his brow. This was not the man who'd issued lazy promises to take away all her worries. This was the man who was worth billions, who took over businesses like most people changed underwear.

'It won't take me long.' She gestured towards her bedroom door. 'Raf's still sleeping. I didn't want to disturb him.'

Gabe's eyes narrowed. 'We're leaving soon. Disturbing him is inevitable.' And then, after a pause, 'I'll hold him.'

Abby jerked her attention to his face. 'Seriously?'

Gabe's smile was slightly mocking. 'He's my son, *no*?'

She arched a brow, her surprise obvious. But he was right, and hadn't she wanted him to be a good father?

When she walked into her bedroom, it was to discover that the little boy was already stirring, his back arched, his head pushed upwards and his lips pouting as he stretched the sleep away. She smiled instinctively and pulled him into her arms, pressing a kiss to his soft little head. 'Your daddy's here, Raf.'

Gabe was watching her initially when she stepped into the lounge, but then all of his attention, the full force of him, was channelled towards their son.

Abby didn't have a camera handy, but she didn't need one anyway. She would always, always remember the tortured look on Gabe's face in that moment. He wore an expression of such deep feelings, such pain, that she almost forgot all the reasons she had to keep him at a distance.

She almost forgot the way he'd treated her after the night they'd shared—she almost forgot the way he'd ignored her, refused to allow her to apologise or explain, refused to give her the dignity of so much as a simple conversation so that she could tell him about the baby.

She almost forgot that he was, in many ways, the enemy.

She longed instead to wrap her arms around his waist, to lift up onto her tiptoes and press a kiss against his lips. To whisper into his mouth that he could make up for the three months he'd missed—that he had a lifetime to be in his child's life and it was all about to start.

She didn't, though.

Sanity and the reality of who they were to one another prevented her from weakening, even a little. She handed Raf to Gabe, careful not to touch him more than she had to in order to effect the transfer, and then stepped back with a crisp nod. 'I won't be long.'

Gabe didn't answer; she couldn't have said if he'd even heard. He was in his own world—just him and Raf. She watched, and tried her darndest to ignore the strange prickling impression that she was an outsider.

* * *

Abby had grown up with money, she was used to this rarefied way of living, and yet she still felt a tremble of anxiety as she moved up the metallic stairs and into the body of the private jet.

There were markers of understated luxury everywhere she looked, from the sleek white leather seats to the highly polished woodgrain meeting table and the small cinema space at the back of the plane.

It took her a moment to realise that they weren't alone. Three women and one man were seated at the back of the plane, and there were the two men in dark suits who'd lifted the luggage from the car.

Gabe walked towards the people at the rear of the plane, his grim expression not lifting. For lack of knowing what else she should do, Abby fell into step behind him.

One of the women stood at his approach, a smile on her face. Abby liked her instantly. She was tall and slim, in her forties, Abby would have guessed, and while she was dressed in beautiful clothes, her glossy brown hair was braided down her back and she wore no make-up. She had a nice face. Smile lines and bright eyes that spoke of a quick wit and good humour.

'Hello, little one,' she cooed as Gabe approached and, to Abby's surprise, he passed their son to the other woman.

She watched, trying to make sense of this development before reacting.

'You must be Abigail,' the other woman said, her tone soft, her eyes not leaving Raf's face.

'Abby, please,' Abigail murmured, her voice sounding hoarse. She cleared her throat softly.

'I'm Monique.'

Perhaps reading the look of confusion on Abby's face, Gabe explained, 'I have engaged Monique as Raf's nanny. This is her team.' He nodded to the others. Apparently, they didn't need names.

But Abby barely noticed. How could she? Not when the hiring of a nanny was a reality still detonating in her brain.

'What did you say?' Anger fuelled the words. She didn't particularly want to argue in front of the nice-seeming nanny, but her maternal instincts were twisting inside her.

And he understood; he easily read the emotions that were about to burst from her. His eyes sparked with Abby's and he put a hand on the small of her back, his touch none-too-gentle.

'Come with me.'

He propelled her down the aisle and only the knowledge that no harm could befall Raf when she was only on the other side of the aircraft meant she went with Gabe without complaint.

But as soon as they were far enough away she

whipped around and hissed, 'You can't just hire a nanny without talking to me!'

His expression was unyielding. 'Why not?'

'Because!' Finally she gave into the impulse to lash out at him, lifting a hand and pushing his chest, hard. He didn't move. Not even a little. He was like a stone wall to her ricocheting emotions.

'Because that's something I want to be consulted on. Who is this woman? What experience does she have with children? You're asking me to hand my son over to a stranger! I should have been able to review her résumé. Besides, how good can she be if you were able to organise her within a *day* of finding out you have a son? Or do you just keep nannies waiting in the wings in case you discover you have a secret baby somewhere?' Her brain kept firing and new possibilities detonated sharply. 'Oh, God, do you have other children? Has this happened before?' Abby felt light-headed, and not just because of her tirade but because her palms were resting against Gabe's chest and her fingertips were tingling with the contact, sending little barbs of electricity through her veins, making her knees tremble.

She didn't want to be aware of him physically! Not in this moment! Not when she should be simply enraged.

'No,' he responded, his own word filled with barely restrained anger. 'Raf is a first for me.'

'So?' Abby wasn't placated. 'Where did you find this woman? What are her credentials? How dare you hire someone without taking the time to make sure it was safe or right?' Her eyes shifted to the back of the plane, but thick grey curtains had been drawn, partitioning the staff from Abby and Gabe.

He wrapped his fingers around her wrists, removing her hands from his chest and holding her arms down by her side. 'He is my son. I would *never* do anything that might put him in harm's way.'

'Like engaging a nanny you know *nothing* about?' Abby retaliated, her gaze smarting.

'Monique has worked for the Italian ambassador for six years. I have met her a number of times in that capacity and she comes with excellent references. Her security clearance is the highest imaginable. I trust her implicitly, or I wouldn't have hired her.'

He released his grip on her wrists and stepped backwards, the distance and lack of physical contact immediately frustrating to Abby.

His reasonable response was like a pin popping her anger and yet still she said, 'You should have spoken to me about it. This kind of thing should be my decision too.'

'And?' he said, crossing his arms over his chest, drawing her attention to the breadth of his torso—

a torso that had been naked above her, that made her ache to feel his body weight once more. She looked away, her mouth suddenly dry. 'Would you have wanted her, Abigail?'

'I'm raising my son,' she said wearily, taking a step back from him, finding a seat and easing herself into it. She curled her legs up beneath her and gnawed on her lower lip, the deluge of emotions that was flooding her quite unwelcome.

'Yes.' He took the seat opposite, his long legs spread between them. 'And you are raising him still. It is not a crime to have professional help.'

Tears clogged her throat and she was afraid of speaking in case he heard the emotions in her voice.

'If you decide, after a month or two, that you don't want that help, I am open to re-evaluating the situation.'

It was a concession she hadn't expected. Abby flicked her glance to him, but whatever she'd been about to say flew from her head. He was looking at her lips, focused intently on them, and her pulse began to drum hard and hot, filling her ears, her body, gushing through her in a way that made her insides clench together. Warmth flooded her and she held her breath.

His eyes lifted briefly to hers and heat seared her, and then his attention moved lower, as if drawn of its own accord. She was wearing a shapeless sweater and a pair of jeans, hardly the stuff of expert seduction, and yet, the way his eyes lingered on the soft curves of her breasts, she felt as though she were wearing the latest designer lingerie.

But when he returned his attention to her face, a face that was flushed courtesy of his slow, possessive scrutiny, there was nothing but determined resolve in his look. Nothing to indicate he'd been at all affected by his languid inspection. Whereas Abby felt as if she might need an ice-cold shower to get her wayward thoughts under control…

CHAPTER FIVE

GABE STARED AT the snow-covered fields on either side of the car and, beyond them, the twinkling night sky. His lips were set in a grim line of determination and his mind was focused on avoidance.

Avoiding the consequences of what he'd just manoeuvred.

Avoiding the realities of marriage to a woman like Abigail—a woman he'd sworn he never wanted to see again.

Avoiding the fact she was still fast asleep in the seat opposite, her pale blonde hair like gold across one shoulder, her body languid even in repose, so that he wanted to stare, but to stare only as a prelude to touching her.

'Abigail.' He spoke with a coldness that was completely at odds with the thoughts that had been simmering through his body, tightening him, hardening him, making him remember the softness of her breasts between his palms.

She stirred a little, but remained asleep.

'Abigail.' More loudly, more emphatic, as they passed the turn-off for Fiamatina, the small village at the foot of his land. She blinked her eyes open slowly at first, relaxed, unguarded, and for a few moments she frowned with apparent confusion. Then she looked at him and straightened instantly, her expression wary, her body on alert.

'Where's Raf?'

Her jumper had risen up a little, exposing an inch or so of flesh at her waist. He looked at it without even realising what he was doing until she reached down and straightened the fabric, clearing her throat. 'Gabe?'

He couldn't mistake the desire that was running rampant through his system. That he still wanted her physically was a complication he needed like a hole in the head. 'In the car behind.'

'The car behind?'

'You were asleep,' he said with a shrug. 'I didn't want him to wake you.'

Abby's eyes flicked to the window, then back to Gabe. 'You shouldn't have done that. I don't... How long have I been asleep?'

'A few hours. You drifted off about an hour before we landed.'

She stared at him, surprise obvious. 'I don't even remember landing.' Her cheeks flushed. 'Or getting into the car.'

'I carried you.'

Her body had been soft and warm against his, pliant to his touch, and she'd made a small sigh as she'd curled in closer, her lips so close to his throat that he could feel her breath.

'Why?' She pressed back further in her seat and

crossed her arms. Her body language told him she wanted to be anywhere but in his car, anywhere but with him.

'You were obviously exhausted,' he said softly.

She didn't answer, nor did she see the way his eyes stayed focused on her face for several long seconds.

'We're almost home.'

Her eyes swept shut at that pronouncement and a twist of guilt tightened in his gut. He'd made this happen, and it had been the right thing to do. He was nothing like his own father; he was the complete opposite. He'd proved that by manoeuvring Abigail into his life, into this marriage.

He'd meant what he'd said in New York: he would take care of her; he would take away her worries.

He would be everything his father wasn't—Raf would know how much Gabe loved him; that fact would never be in doubt.

This was the *right* decision, he reassured himself, ignoring the insistent pounding of doubt.

Abby couldn't help the small gasp that escaped her when the car pulled off the road and began to ascend a narrow, curving drive. It was night-time, but against the black velvet sky she could make out enormous pine trees capped in white, their big, fluffy branches cloud-like with snow. In the distance, there looked to be a small village, perhaps a town, the buildings glowing warm and golden. The car moved higher and, as they rounded a bend, a scene that could have been straight from one of Abby's girlhood fantasies lifted almost as if magically from the earth.

'It's a castle,' she whispered, moving closer to the window so that she could see better. The building looked to be quite ancient. In the light that was cast by the moon she could see it was built of stone, perhaps a yellow-coloured stone? It was four storeys high, with a central turret and lots of little balconies. She could make out the detail more clearly as they drove nearer—the castle was well-illuminated. In fact, it looked as though every light was on, the place appearing almost to glow.

'You live here?' She turned to face him, her surprise obvious.

His nod was a short confirmation.

'But it's so beautiful…'

'You have not realised I like beautiful things?'

She had no reason to suspect he was talking about her and yet her cheeks warmed and her heart tripped in her chest. 'I just hadn't expected this.'

'What did you expect?'

She shrugged. 'Some super-modern apartment in Rome?'

'I have a place in Rome,' he conceded with a dip of his head. 'I stay there for work sometimes.'

'But you prefer it here,' she said softly, turning to face him.

He studied her for a long moment before shrugging. 'It's quiet.'

'It's…lovely.' The word felt insufficient, hugely so. But it was also very, very apt. Beauty was *everywhere*. She was in a snow-covered wonderland, like the snow globe her mother had brought back one year after a concert season in Vienna.

A moment after the car had drawn to a stop the door was pulled open but, before Abby could step from the car, Gabe put a hand out, arresting her with his touch. It was just a light contact, his fingers pressed to her knee. Abby froze instantly, turning to face him with eyes that were huge in her face.

'It's cold out,' he said thickly, reaching beside him and handing her a black woollen overcoat.

'Thank you.' Just a murmur when, inside, her heart was racing at the thoughtfulness of the gesture. She was less grateful when she pulled the coat on and realised it was his. It swam on her; she could easily have fitted herself into the thing twice. Worse than that, it was filled with his intoxicatingly masculine fragrance so that her hormones tripped in her body, responding instantly to the memories of their night together, reminding her of the way they'd made love.

She ignored the recollections, focusing her attention instead on the castle. She was no expert in Italian history but she would have guessed the castle to be fifteenth or sixteenth century. It looked too rustic to have been influenced by the Renaissance movement, though that didn't mean it wasn't beautiful. In fact, it was the most beautiful thing Abby had ever seen. The windows were cathedral in shape and the door, at the very middle of the castle, was at least twice Abby's height and made of thick, ancient wood. She'd put money on the wood having been sourced from one of these enormous pines—the forest that surrounded the castle must be hundreds of years old too. She breathed in deeply and tasted Christmas.

It was an odd thought for a woman who hadn't celebrated the holiday in more than the most perfunctory of ways for many years. But if she could write Christmas as a fairy tale it would be set somewhere like this. A bird flew overhead, a night bird with wide wings and a soft song. Abby's eyes were drawn upwards, following its progress and then remaining on the jewel-encrusted sky.

No matter how beautiful the setting, Abby needed to remember that it wasn't, in fact, a fairy tale. Being here with Gabe might have been the answer to many of her problems but she was pretty sure it would bring with it a whole raft of new worries. She just couldn't bring herself to deal with them yet.

The crunching of tyres called her attention back to earth and the present moment. She spun, the jacket warm around her, to see a mini-van arrive. Monique stepped out first, Raf nestled in her arms.

He was awake, but looking perfectly calm in the face of all these changes. He was still so tiny, just a very wrapped-up little bundle with a tiny face poking out the top.

Monique smiled at Abby, crossing to her. 'He did very well on the flight, Abigail. Barely a peep, except when we landed, and a pacifier soothed him right back.'

Abby nodded, though she couldn't help feeling like the worst mother ever for not even hearing her child's distress. Raf hadn't been interested in pacifiers before, though she'd tried to introduce them, to buy peace and quiet when he was at his most inconsolable. A niggling doubt that maybe she hadn't tried hard enough, or simply hadn't known enough, spread like wildfire.

She reached out a finger, touching her little one's forehead, and, though it was absurd and made no sense, she didn't try to take him from the nanny. For some strange reason, she almost felt as if she didn't have any right.

Perhaps sensing her ambivalence, Monique smiled kindly. 'I will take him inside and bathe him. Would you like me to give him his bottle or…?'

'No.' Abby shook her head, grateful that the other woman seemed to understand that she was generally a very hands-on mother. 'I'll do that.'

Monique nodded and moved back to the others; they went as a group towards the castle but Abby held back a little, watching as they disappeared through the enormous timber doors.

She felt balanced on a precipice, one foot in her old life and this new existence beckoning her. It was a reality that shimmered like a reflection in a pond; she could see it and fathom it, but its edges were rippled and the exact nature of it was too hard to properly understand.

If she took a step, and then another, would she disappear for ever beneath the surface? Would she be a part of this world only?

She swallowed, thinking of Manhattan. The father who'd disowned her years ago. Oh, he'd made it official only recently, but his heart had turned cold to Abby much earlier than that.

She thought of her apartment, the tiny space and life she had tried to carve out for herself. She thought of the fridge that was full of bills and emptied of food, and the heating that was too costly to use, and the difficulties of juggling the need to work with trying to make everything good for Raf, and she swept her eyes shut, as if she could dissolve the image of America so easily.

'Come.' His voice was gravel. 'I'll show you around.'

Snow was thick on the ground everywhere except for the driveway that led to the front entrance; someone must have cleared it very recently because it was already beginning to fall again. Abby paused at the door, turning around to survey the setting once more. The village twinkled in the distance, the pine trees loomed large, fragrant with their alpine scent, and the air was so clear and bright that Abby would swear she could make out the shape of the stars. It was a place that seemed almost to have been carved from heaven.

'Well?' His impatient word cut through the serenity of the moment. 'I know you've been living in an ice box but perhaps we could move inside before freezing to death.'

'I'm sorry I'm not moving fast enough for you.' The words were laced with tart acidity. 'I just wanted to get my bearings.'

He ground his teeth.

'That is Fiamatina, a small village that formed around this castle. The closest city is Turin, about two hours that way. The alps, obviously—' and he nodded to his right. When she turned, she gasped again. They *were* obvious and yet she hadn't yet noticed them, so awestruck had she been by the castle. If she'd thought the sky glistening, she had been ill prepared for the sight of the Italian alps, snow-covered, on a bright moonlit night. They looked to have been cast from silver and diamond dust, yet, for all their beauty, there was something simultaneously frightening about their dramatic, looming presence. They were hard and defined, sharp against the night sky. Abby ran her gaze across them, as far as the eye could see in one direction; her shiver was involuntary.

'Do you have your bearings now, Abigail?'

'Yes,' she responded sharply, though she would have liked to stand out there for longer.

Gabe was right to chivvy her along; Raf would be hungry and she was desperate to hold her little boy, to cuddle him and reassure them both that, for all the changes, life was still normal; they were still together.

A family.

Just like Gabe had said.

He walked into the castle as though it were completely normal, and yet Abby needed another moment to take stock, this time of the interior. The entranceway was high, with vaulted ceilings, and all of it mosaic—the floors a cream and white swirling pattern and the walls with an emphasis on black and grey. There were armchairs to one side, creating a sort of lounge foyer that wouldn't have been out of place in an exclusive hotel. At some point the building had obviously been heavily modernised. The lighting was like an art gallery, all concealed and elegant, and the heating was excellent. She shrugged out of her coat, surrendering to the cosy warmth of a building that was so utterly enormous. The staircase in the middle of the entrance hall, though made of old terracotta tiles, looked to have been remodelled at some point in recent years.

'There is a kitchen here, though you will not need to cook, of course. I have a team of domestics who take care of castle operations.'

Her father had never believed in servants. They'd only had a nanny when she'd been younger, and a cleaner as she'd got older. He'd said he didn't like the way it felt to have people hovering around his home, touching his things, watching him breathe. She wondered if she'd ever get used to the omnipresence of an invisible brigade of helpers.

'I will show you the back of the house tomorrow; there is a garden you might like to explore. Somewhere Raf can play. It is fenced, so you need not worry he will escape.'

'Okay.' She nodded, but her head was swimming. The house—no, it wasn't a house—the *castle* was sumptuous.

He led her up the staircase, moving quickly, so she almost had to jog to keep up with him. At the landing, he split in one direction and she followed him. It was on the tip of her tongue to implore him to slow down when he did just that, so she had to halt abruptly or risk bumping into him.

'This is Raf's room.' He stepped back to allow her to precede him, and his eyes glowed with an emotion she couldn't immediately understand.

It was defiance, she realised, when she stepped over the threshold and saw the way Gabe had furnished it. He was telling her that he was right—that he had been right to insist she accompany him.

Abby had no idea what the room had been in the past, but it was now a child's paradise. There was a bassinet and a cot, a small chair—something he wouldn't need for many months yet. There was a baby jumper, a walker, shelves and shelves lined with age-appropriate toys, a rocking chair, a narrow bed that an adult could use. Abby walked around the room, her breath held as she fingered many of the objects, her mind sagging when she tried to calculate what this must have cost him. A year's rent for her, certainly.

There was a doorway on one side; she went through it and discovered a large bathroom to one side and a bedroom to the other.

'The nannies will take it in turns to be on duty overnight. Whoever is watching Raf will sleep here.'

'And the bed in his room?' she asked softly, her eyes swept shut.

He shrugged. 'If he's sick. Has nightmares.'

It was the kind of thoughtful inclusion she wouldn't have expected of him.

'How did you *arrange* all this so quickly? It must have been hard to source so many items…'

'Not particularly.'

Of course it wasn't. For someone like Gabe, this would have been easy. Just a click of his fingers, a flex of his wallet, and all was arranged.

'Where's my room?'

He regarded her for several seconds before turning away and stalking through Raf's comfortable suite. Abby followed. Gabe walked past several doors that must have led to other bedrooms, and eventually he paused at the end of the hallway.

Until he opened the door, Abby hadn't realised she'd been holding her breath, fully expecting— hoping—that Gabe would insist they share a bedroom…and a bed! Deep, deep down, she'd been preparing for the likelihood and, in the back of her mind, trying to fathom how she would respond to that.

But the room he gestured towards was definitely not his. It was furnished in neutral décor, for one thing, with a couple of flower arrangements on the bedside table and a dressing table. It was devoid of personal details.

'My room,' she said with a confident nod, as if telling herself, reassuring herself.

'My own is next door,' he said, the words giving no indication that this affected him in any way.

But for Abby? Knowing he would be so close made her heart throb inside her and her pulse pounded in her veins, rushing hard and fast, demanding attention. Colour bloomed in her cheeks and when she lifted her eyes to Gabe he was watching her intently.

'Unless you'd prefer to share my room,' he prompted silkily, and Abby's knees began to tremble.

One night.

Her only night with a man.

The feelings he'd invoked had tormented her, the memories strong and vivid in her mind, demanding more, craving more. But there'd been no more. No Gabe, only memories.

And now?

She blinked at him, her expression unknowingly panic-stricken. But it wasn't fear of being with him; it was fear of showing him just how much she wanted and needed that! It was fear of the fact she did want him, even now. That, no matter what she'd promised to herself, she knew she wanted Gabe in a way she couldn't—wouldn't—ignore. Did that make her foolish or brave? And what point did a definition serve?

She was hungry for him, desperate for his touch, despite knowing she might very well regret succumbing to that hunger. She felt instinct take over, changing the course of her determination with ease.

'Relax, *tempesta*. It was a joke. I think we both know one night together was one night too many.'

Gabe was just a boy again and his mother, Marina, was dying. Not of any illness, but because of the drugs she slid into her veins until she was no longer coherent. She was dying and he couldn't save her.

He remembered the fear of those times, the pain of trying to hug her and make her laugh. Of having her bat him away from her legs, push at him and say, with fury, 'You are just like *him*!'

How she'd hated Gabe when she'd been high. Gabe was like his father, Lorenzo, and that was something his mother couldn't forgive.

Raf wouldn't know that pain. He wouldn't know the anger that was a by-product of paternal estrangement. He wouldn't have a father who rejected his mother and made her miserable. Raf would be spared what Gabe had seen and lived— Raf would have everything, including a mother who was cared for by his father.

Gabe just had to find a way to forgive Abigail for who she was and what she'd done—he wouldn't let their son feel the measure of Gabe's antipathy. At least, he hoped he wouldn't.

CHAPTER SIX

THE DREAM HAD disturbed him and some time around dawn he woke, sweat beading on his brow, his eyes heavy with angry emotions. Jogging was something Gabe had long indulged in, particularly when he needed to blow off steam. He ran for six miles and then came back to the castle, restless and as irritable as he'd been for days.

Without knowing what he was doing or where he was going, he found his feet moving towards the stairs and then taking him upwards. One hand curled around the balustrade, part securing him, part deterring him.

At the door to their son's room, he hesitated only a moment before pushing in. The child was awake. Lying in his crib, his huge eyes open and staring at the mobile that hung above it.

A powerful instinct fired inside Gabe's gut. Possession, fierce pride and love. Yes, love. He'd never felt it before but now it flooded through him, unmistakable and all-consuming. He hovered above the cot, unsure what to do at first.

Then Raf made a gurgling noise and lifted an arm, his eyes locked to Gabe's, and Gabe followed his instincts, reaching down into the crib and lifting the little boy.

He made a guttural noise of surrender as he cradled Raf to his chest, pressing his face to the boy's sweet, downy head, breathing in his intoxicating baby fragrance.

'You're my son,' he whispered, the words not entirely even. 'And I am going to take all the care in the world of you.' He breathed in once more. 'I love you.'

It was a freezing cold morning and Abigail had risen at dawn. In part owing to jetlag and in part owing to dreams that had been causing her nerve-endings to reverberate, making her ache to do something really, really stupid.

She'd tiptoed past Gabe's room, even when she'd been tempted to push his door inwards and climb into his bed. To seek his body, not caring for how pathetic that made her. How needy and desperate.

There was only one activity that ever helped soothe Abby in times of stress. She'd had to abandon ballet for the last few months of her pregnancy and since Raf had been born she hadn't had much energy for anything other than a bit of stretching. But an urge to go back to her roots now drove her with a wild desperation.

She didn't need much. Just a room that was lightly furnished, a bit of floor space and privacy, and she would have put money on this castle having something to fit the bill *somewhere*.

The perfect room happened to be just opposite the kitchen. A space that might have been a sunroom at one point and which now offered an almost blank canvas. Just a few chairs against one wall, glass doors that opened onto a deck and views of the alps in every direction. She ignored the beauty outside. Looking out only reminded her of where she was—and why—and she needed to forget for a moment. She loaded up a piece from *The Nutcracker Suite* and stretched for the first few minutes, and then she closed her eyes and let the music wash over her, sweeping her into a trance-like state, filling her with a sense of who she was, who her mother had been, what she'd loved about ballet. She danced and felt her worries shift away; she felt safety and security, reassurance and bliss.

She danced the entire song, and then another, but, as the third began to play, something on the periphery of her vision caught her attention and she spun sharply, breaking a pirouette mid-way with surprise, to find Gabe watching her.

No. Staring at her, as though he could eat her with his eyes, his attention finely homed in on every single minuscule shift of her body. A *frisson* of awareness rushed through her. She ignored it, staring back at him unapologetically, trying desperately to match the coldness he could so easily convey.

'Did you want something?' she asked impishly, crossing her arms over her chest, glad she hadn't gone with her first instinct and pulled on her old leotard and tights.

'What are you doing?'

The question was a strange one. Did he really not recognise ballet?

He frowned thoughtfully, shaking his head, as though he realised the stupidity of what he'd said. 'You're a ballerina?'

'No.' Abby remembered the angry conversations with her father, his remonstrations at her 'quitting'. 'I just like to dance.'

'Is it not the same thing?'

'No.' The word held a bone-deep finality. She wasn't going to discuss the career she might have had. Nor the way her father had taken her decision not to pursue it as some kind of personal affront— a perceived rejection of Abby's mother—instead of what it really was: Abby's realisation that she wanted different things from life.

'You...move as though you are part of the song.'

Abby's eyes swept shut. She had been told often enough that she was gifted, and by a variety of people, to know that it was true. That had only added to the outrage at her decision to walk away from the stage.

'Thank you.' It was a curt dismissal.

He blinked, as though clearing his mind of the

vision of her dancing. 'I am going into Fiamatina. Do you need anything?'

'The village?' she asked, a natural curiosity twisting inside her.

'*Sì.*'

Abigail eyed him warily. 'I'd like to go with you.' It would mean a car trip with Gabe, but the chance to explore was something she didn't want to resist. The lure of a snow-topped Italian village did something strange to her tummy.

'Fine. If you wish,' he said, shrugging his shoulders in the same indolent manner he'd employed the night before. 'But I'm leaving soon. Get ready.'

Abby shot daggers at his retreating back; his high-handed manner did funny things to her tummy and knees, making her ache to run up to him and turn him around and demand that he not be so cold to her when she knew a flame was going to combust between them.

'Get ready,' she mimicked under her breath, rolling her big green eyes as she moved through the castle, noting details she hadn't seen earlier. Ancient bricks that formed a vaulted ceiling in the corridors, walls that had been rendered at some point, that were now a charming mix of stone and concrete, walls that told stories. Windows framed views of the alps, snow-covered and magical, each vista like a postcard. She drifted towards one, staring out for a moment, mesmerised by the view.

Was this little slice of heaven on earth really to be her home?

She closed her eyes and breathed in deeply, trying to remember the bedroom in her father's house, the cafés she'd go to for brunch at the weekend, the sound of New York traffic and commuters, the smell of diesel and bitumen heavy in the air; it all seemed so far away.

There wasn't time for reflection; she kept going, taking one wrong turn in the enormous castle before finding her way to the corridor that led to their bedrooms. She paused at Raf's door, listening for noises, and smiled when she heard voices.

She pushed in without knocking and found one of Monique's staff changing Raf's nappy, smiling down at him with all the adoration a mother could wish from someone who was entrusted with their child's care.

'Good morning,' she said, smiling. Raf turned his head. He was only young but already strong and alert, and a big toothless smile appeared on his face, digging dimples into his cheeks.

'Buongiorno,' the young girl said. 'I'm Rosa.'

She was obviously a native Italian, her accent heavy even on the single word 'I'm'.

'Abby.' Abigail stroked Raf's head, smiling back

at him, before placing a kiss on his brow. 'How did he sleep?'

'He slept well,' Rosa answered, lifting Raf off the changing table, cradling him to her hip. 'And now he is going to eat. Would you like to give him his bottle?'

Guilt sliced through Abby and for a moment she wondered if she was doing the wrong thing to abandon her son, even if for only a couple of hours. Yet he seemed so happy, and she wouldn't be long. Besides, if this was to be their home, the sooner she got to grips with their locale, the better she'd be able to make them truly comfortable here.

'I'm on my way to Fiamatina,' she said, shaking her head regretfully. Mother guilt, she'd felt it often, always agonising over whether she was making the right decisions for her child. 'You'll call me if there are any problems?'

'Of course! Raf is a very contented baby, though. We'll be fine.'

Abby nodded, but she was thinking of how difficult he had been in New York, how he had seemed far from content on many occasions. Before she escaped to her own room to ready herself for the trip, she reached for Raf and snuggled him close to her chest, wrapping her arms around him, pressing a kiss to his forehead and breathing him in.

This was all for him. Being here with Gabe, living in the lion's den, that was because she knew Raf deserved what Gabe could provide.

She had to make this work.

'I'll be back in a few hours.' She returned Raf to Rosa and prepared to face the morning.

There was a petulant child inside Abby who wanted to dally over getting ready but, alas, she'd never been someone who took time over her appearance. Besides, there was an excitement coiling inside her, as if she was about to set off on an adventure, to discover the village at the foot of the castle. She showered, marvelling at the heat, not only of the water but of the bathroom, as well. Underfloor warmth greeted her bare feet when she stepped out of the shower—it must have been triggered by the lights, she supposed. She dressed in a pair of jeans and a shirt, pulling on a big grey sweater and a bright pink scarf before reaching for the only jacket she'd brought, a black knee-length coat that buttoned up to her neck.

Gabe was waiting at the bottom of the enormous staircase, the elegant seating area to his left glowing with the milky sunshine from outside. As with before, in the morning light she was able to observe much more of the castle's details than she'd been capable of doing after the strange discombobulation of the day before. The stairs were slightly uneven, worn through the middle by centuries of use. The railing was softened by touch as well, so that she slid her hands over hundreds of years of other peoples' lives, and a shiver ran through her.

But when she reached the bottom and her eyes met Gabe's, all thoughts of the castle and its provenance skittered from her brain. There was only him and her. Even the air seemed somewhat thin, making breathing difficult.

'You will be cold,' he said, eyeing her coat.

It wasn't what she'd expected him to say. 'I'm fine.'

'It's below zero…'

'It's not like I'm not used to the cold,' she interrupted. 'I grew up in New York.'

'Fine,' he said with a shrug, but his obvious disapproval irked her. He was so superior, so arrogant, she yearned to take him down a peg or two.

'Our son is fine, by the way. Thanks for asking. Your concern is truly touching, particularly given the way you uprooted us from our lives so unceremoniously.'

His brows lifted and an electrical current surged from him to her. 'I'm well aware he is fine. I gave him a bottle before coming in search of you this morning.'

Just like a tower being demolished, Abby's moral high ground gave way beneath her, leaving her feeling churlish. Worse, she felt like someone who'd used their baby to score points, something she'd sworn she'd never do.

Refusing to apologise, she stared at a point over Gabe's shoulder. 'Rosa said he slept well.'

Gabe could have continued their spat but he didn't, and she was glad. 'Yes. Perhaps it is the Italian air that agrees with him.'

'Perhaps.'

They walked side by side from the castle, through the enormous wooden door at the front. The icy temperature hit her like a wall. It was *much* colder than she'd expected. The castle had been so cosy she hadn't been able to grasp that beyond its walls was a sub-arctic breeze. She didn't respond visibly though; he didn't need to know he'd been right. Next time she'd have to add another layer or three beneath her coat.

In the daylight, everything was clean and shiny, glowing white against a leaden grey sky. It wasn't snowing, but it had done so overnight. The freshly fallen powder had been recently pushed aside and a sleek black sports car was parked at the foot of the steps. It was exactly the kind of car she would have expected Gabe to drive. Expensive-looking, undoubtedly powerful and very expensive.

She pulled open the passenger door, sliding into the warmth of the vehicle with relief, buckling up and pressing back against the leather of the seat.

A blast of ice-cold air hit Abby as Gabe slid into

the seat beside her, his powerful frame taking all the spare space, his presence a force to be reckoned with and conquered. The engine throbbed when he started it, like a beast beneath them. He steered it away from the house, his driving expert. Once they cleared his long winding driveway and entered the streets there was thick snow, but Gabe and the vehicle had no problem manoeuvring across it.

'You don't need to grip the door as though you are about to die,' he said, tilting his face sidelong to regard her with sardonic amusement before returning his attention to the road. 'You are safe.'

Safe? She didn't feel safe. In the road sense, she did, but the reason her nerve-endings were pulling taut had more to do with the man beside her and the anxiety his proximity kindled within her.

'Have you lived here long?' she asked to ease the tension within her.

He arched a brow, turning his handsome face towards her. 'Small talk?'

'Curiosity,' she corrected. 'If I'm going to marry you, I figure I should know a bit more about you besides the fact you're a judgemental douche.'

'A judgemental douche?' he repeated and, despite the cynicism in his tone, there was the hint of a smile at the corner of his mouth.

'Yes.' Abby wasn't laughing.

He sobered. '*Va bene.*'

'So?' she said after a long moment of silence had stretched between them. He slowed the car to a halt. 'Why have you stopped?'

He jerked his head and Abby followed the direction of his gaze. Two deer were making their way across the road, picking their way slowly through the snow, their inky-black eyes alert as they eyed Gabe's car warily. It looked like a scene from a Christmas movie. All that was missing were bells around their necks and elves at their sides.

'I've lived in the castle about five years.'

'Why? It seems so remote.'

'I like remote.'

'Yes,' she drawled. 'I can see that.' Again, she was sure she saw his lips twitch. The deer moved off the road and Gabe started to accelerate gently, continuing their journey.

'I have a helicopter for when I need to get to my office in Rome.' He frowned and when their eyes met she wondered if he was imagining her in his lobby. Pregnant and desperate to talk to him. Was he remembering the way he'd had Security remove her from the premises? Did he feel guilty? He turned his attention back to the road. 'But I have all the facilities I need to work from here.'

'The castle is amazing,' she agreed. 'I can see why you were drawn to it.'

'I doubt that,' he said under his breath.

'What do you mean?'

He was quiet for a moment. 'It doesn't matter.'

Curiosity exploded inside her. Was there more behind his purchase of the castle? Suddenly, she wanted to know everything. She wanted to pick Gabe's brain, to understand him completely and unequivocally, but she suspected he wouldn't willingly accede to that.

He turned at a large pine tree and the snow-covered road gave way to one that was ever so slightly less so, as though it had been swept clear an hour or so earlier. Just the lightest dusting of white had fallen over it since.

'The castle was the heart of this village. It was once a great agricultural stronghold and supported all of the people who lived here.'

But Abby heard Gabe's words in the very back of her mind. She was leaning forward in her seat, her breath held, as she stared out of the windscreen at Fiamatina. It was, without doubt, the most charming and exquisitely beautiful place she had ever seen. The buildings all looked to be very, very old and, like the castle, they were built of stone. Mostly, they were joined together, forming rows and rows of cottages with ancient windows, creating streets so narrow that two cars couldn't have been accommodated at the same time. In deference to this, or perhaps to allow Abby to see everything they passed, Gabe went slowly, winding the car through street after street. Swathes of greenery were hung between the walls, covered in snow now, giving the Christmas decorations even more of a hint of festivity. The shops they passed were decorated too, and Abby was itching to explore properly.

When Gabe turned the corner again, the village opened into a square with a large Renaissance statue in the centre—the Virgin Mary and Baby Jesus, also topped with snow. A garland had been laid at their feet recently enough that it was still fresh.

Gabe brought the car to a stop. 'I will be a few hours. I presume you will be able to entertain yourself without getting into any trouble, for that short space of time?'

Abby lifted her eyes to his, frustration zipping through her. 'This doesn't exactly look like the kind of place that invites trouble.'

'Still, you are particularly good at finding your way into it,' he said, his words not showing a hint of humour or kindness. 'Try not to seduce any of the local businessmen, *tempesta*. You will not find their secrets worth keeping. Nor their wealth worth having, compared to mine.'

She sucked in an angry breath, her chest burning with the unfairness of his accusation. 'I didn't seduce you...'

He laughed and then shook his head as if sobering with the speed of lightning. He reached across and gripped her chin between his forefinger and thumb. 'You seduced me a year ago, make no mistake. But I have your measure now; you will not find me so foolish again.'

She wanted to tell him to go to hell, that she wouldn't touch him with a ten-foot bargepole for a million dollars, but already her body was making a liar of her, warming beneath his touch, filling with remembered pleasures.

His eyes roamed her face, dark emotions spiralling through them. 'Did you make a habit of doing your father's bidding?'

A soft sigh fell from Abby's lips. 'I love him,' she said simply. 'He's my dad.'

Something flickered in Gabe's expression and he dropped his hand. 'He's a fool.'

Sadness began to ricochet through Abby. 'It's not that simple,' she demurred with a small shake of her head. 'He's just… Since losing Mom, the business is all he has. He's so proud of his company but since Bright Spark came onto the scene it's been so hard for him.'

'My products dominate because they are, simply, better.'

His arrogance was no less galling because it was the truth. 'I'm trying to explain that he would do anything to succeed…'

'Including sending his only child to bed with a man she barely knew.'

'God, don't be so… You make it sound so sleazy,' she said with a shake of her head. 'It wasn't like that.'

'No?' Snow had begun to fall and it was blanketing the windscreen, removing the square from their view and vice versa. In the distance, she could hear beautiful Benedictine-type music, those lovely melodious chants, and she wondered if there was a church nearby.

'What *was* it like then?'

Abby swallowed, drawing her gaze back to Gabe's. 'He just wanted me to find stuff out about Calypso,' she said, her eyes falling away again almost instantly. His fury and contempt were not easy to face. 'The going to bed with you thing was all me.'

'So you remained a virgin until twenty-two, only to fall into bed with someone you barely knew? That sounds unlikely.'

It sounded preposterous. How could she explain that he wasn't like *anyone* she'd ever known? That he had been bone-meltingly perfect and every cell in her body had recognised that they were meant to sleep together, that he was what she'd been waiting for?

The thought was one she certainly didn't appreciate.

Abby wasn't going to share that train of thought with Gabe. He was looking at her with the kind of mockery that made her want to lash out—to diminish what they'd shared in the same way he had.

'I was a twenty-two-year-old virgin,' she heard herself say, laughing. 'I just wanted to sleep with *someone*.' The lie was weird in her mouth but she was glad for it when she saw the way his face paled beneath his tan. Good. 'Anyone would have done, but you happened to be there…'

He swore, bringing his face closer to hers. 'You are not what I thought,' he said darkly.

'No? Well, that's mutual. My dad was definitely right about you.'

If she'd known him better, she would have understood that the wolfish smile on his face held a warning.

'I'm almost certain he was,' Gabe agreed. His face was dangerously close to Abby's but she didn't back down; she barely even noticed. She was lost in his gaze.

'So you slept with me because you wanted to have sex.'

'Yes.'

'Despite having waited…'

'I didn't wait for any magical reason,' she snapped. 'I just didn't get around to it…'

'Until you met me.'

'Look, Gabe.' She aimed for irreverent amusement, but the words sounded strangled. Now that she'd committed to this, she had to keep going. 'I was embarrassed by my virginity, okay? I wanted to be like any other woman my age.'

He stared at her long and hard and then shook his head, his expression cold. 'You failed. You are not like any woman I have ever met.'

CHAPTER SEVEN

GABE SLAMMED THE car door shut with more force than he'd intended. Their argument—her admissions—had got under his skin and he couldn't, for the life of him, say why! He had long since ceased thinking anything but the worst of his son's mother, so why should he be surprised that she'd used him simply to get rid of her unwanted virginity?

Because it hadn't *felt* like that. The night they'd shared had been different for Gabe. Despite the fact he had been with many women in his time, he'd never had the privilege of being a woman's first. That she'd trusted him had meant something to Gabe. How foolish!

She'd had an itch, that was all, and she'd used him to scratch it.

'I've never done this before,' she'd whispered, her eyes not meeting his. Moonlight had filtered into the apartment, casting her naked body in silver dust.

'You've never done what? Slept with a man you've just met?'

She'd shaken her head and then met his gaze, her eyes locking onto his as though drawn to them by threads of biological imperative. 'Slept with any man.'

The confession had robbed him of breath. 'How is that possible?' He'd pulled her closer to his body, seeing the way desire flushed her skin as his arousal pressed hard to her body.

She'd groaned, rolling her hips in an innate instinctive need to be close to him. 'I just didn't get around to it before.'

He'd nodded, an unusual uncertainty shifting through him, causing him to pause. 'We don't have to, Abby. Your first time is…special…a gift.'

'I want to,' she'd whispered, lifting onto her tiptoes to kiss him. 'Please, Gabe. I want you to be my first.'

Liar.

She had told him the truth originally, only he hadn't listened. *I just didn't get around to it before.* That was the real reason for her virginity. For whatever reason, she'd not had sex. That was her choice, just as sleeping with him had been her choice. But it hadn't been a gift; it simply hadn't *mattered* to her.

And now it didn't matter to Gabe. If possible, his opinion of Abigail Howard sank even lower. His mouth was a grim line as he stormed through Fiamatina. There was nothing for it; he would marry her but he certainly didn't relish the prospect. Not one bit.

* * *

The condemnation rang in her ears—and there was no other way to describe the tone of his voice, the words he'd chosen. He hadn't meant the parting shot—that she was unlike any woman he'd ever known—as a compliment. He had intended to hurt her. Or perhaps he hadn't; perhaps he'd simply been speaking his mind and it was Abby's feelings that were making her vulnerable to his judgement.

His words consumed her, so that she walked through the village for at least an hour before realising that she was freezing cold, and also that she'd been so wrapped up in her tortured reflections she'd barely seen a thing. With a soft sigh of frustration, she pushed Gabe from her mind, or resolved to try, and made herself look at her surroundings. She'd wandered in a circle and was now in a street that was at the end of the square where he'd parked his car. He'd told her to meet him back there in two hours, meaning she had a little over an hour left to explore.

Warming up was also a priority. The street she was in was lined with shops. A few were closed but the third she passed was open and she pushed inside, realising when she entered that it had a collection of gifts. Nothing gaudy or touristic though; the items assembled were all of the highest quality.

'*Ciao, signorina!*' the shopkeeper called from behind a counter. Abby looked in his direction with a small smile. He was in his fifties, pleasingly rotund and short, with a thick white beard that fell to the second button of the grey shirt he wore. Red suspenders held his trousers in place. He was the picture of an Italian Father Christmas.

He said something in Italian and Abby shook her head. 'I'm sorry, I only speak English.' Something she'd have to remedy if she was going to make a go of life here.

'American?'

'*Sì*.'

'Welcome.' His English was heavily accented, his smile bright. ''Ave a look around. If I can help, you say, okay?'

She nodded. 'Okay.'

The shop was a marvel. She looked at statues first, tiny enough to fit in the palm of her hand, carved out of marble, all the details and intricacies perfect despite their miniature size. There were different coloured candles and Christmas ornaments made of wood, the like of which she'd always associated with Germany. Nativity scenes mostly, set at the base of elaborate shapes that, when candles were lit, would spin a fan at the top, causing the arrangement to move. Music boxes were also in evidence.

'It's all so beautiful,' she said to herself.

'Eh?'

'*Bella*,' Abby supplied, waving her hand towards the shelves. Her eyes fell on something in the corner and she moved towards it with a greedy hunger for everything this quaint little shop could offer.

The shelf was laden with Christmas decorations, but unlike anything she'd ever seen. They were spherical in shape, made of blown glass so fine that it was almost like a wisp of cloud. Each had been etched with a festive scene, some of the nativity, others with Santa and his elves, and inside each there was a bell, so tiny that when Abby lifted one ornament it made the most beautiful little noise, almost like a sigh.

'Oh...' She turned to the man, wishing she could convey to him how perfect they were.

But he understood. '*Aspetti*,' he said, then his brow beetled. 'Wait. Wait.'

He disappeared behind a thick velvet curtain and when he returned it was with a younger woman at his side. She wore an apron and had her dark hair pinned up into a loose bun. She brought with her the faint hint of gingerbread and a kind smile.

'My daughter,' the man said, his pride obvious. Abby's heart lurched. When was the last time her father had looked at her with anything like pride? Affection? Never.

'*Ciao*,' the woman said. 'You are American?' She spoke English more comfortably.

'Yes.' Abby nodded.

'You like the decorations?'

Abby nodded. 'They're…exquisite.'

The man said something and the daughter translated Abby's summation. He smiled. *'Sì, certamente.'*

He seemed gratified by Abby's appreciation.

'They're unique to this area,' the woman said. 'When our village formed, some craftsmen from Murano were amongst the first townspeople. They brought their skills with them, and these became the specialty. Each… How you say it? Father to son to father to son?'

'Generation?' Abby supplied after a moment.

'Yes! Each generation has learned from their father. There are only three people left in the village who make them, and they make only fifty each per year—to keep them special.'

Abby doubted she'd ever seen anything more beautiful.

'They are said to bring luck and wishes,' the woman continued. 'But I don't know if this is true. I think they are just pretty.'

Abby nodded her agreement. She could see them on a big green tree, with fine fairy lights twinkling amongst them, making them sparkle with tiny reflections. Though Abby hadn't celebrated Christmas with any degree of enthusiasm since her mother had died, she now felt a jolt of enthusiasm at the prospect. Why shouldn't she dec-

orate a tree this year? It was, after all, Raf's first
Christmas and that meant something, didn't it?
'How much are they?'

'Quanta costa?' the woman asked her father.

He named an amount that had Abby's heart
sinking. They were beautiful and rare—what had
she expected? She thought of her bank balance
with a hint of desperation.

'I'll take two,' she said, thinking it was still an
extravagance she could ill afford.

'Two,' the woman said with a nod, lifting her
fingers to her father to translate. 'Enjoy them.' She
waved her hand in farewell, disappearing back
behind the curtain to the business of baking and
domestic happiness.

The shopkeeper wrapped the decorations with
care and placed them in a bag. When she handed
over the money, he gripped her hand and smiled,
a smile that was filled with genuine care. 'They
give luck, *sì?* You have the luck now.'

Abby nodded, though of course she didn't believe in such superstitions. In any event, she'd need
more than luck to make it through her marriage to
Gabe Arantini unscathed.

She checked the clock in the town square—she
still had fifteen minutes to spare. She pulled her
coat tighter around her waist and walked down the
street, looking in the shop windows—not risking
going into any others! She couldn't *afford* to suc-

cumb to the charming wares of this part of the world.

She was freezing cold though. She jammed her free hand into her pocket and moved back towards the square. The alps loomed large in the background, so beautiful, like something out of Narnia. There was a heavy sense of magic and spells in the air of Fiamatina; even the people she saw seemed to be otherworldly, somehow.

'You're finished?' Gabe's voice came from behind her and Abby turned to see that he was carrying several shopping bags and wearing a mask of disapproval. A hangover from their conversation in the car?

'Yes,' she said with regret. If she were dressed more appropriately, she would have wanted to stay all day.

He nodded, clicking a button so that the trunk of his car pushed itself open. 'You're cold.'

He lifted something out of one of the bags. 'Here.'

It was a coat, clotted cream in colour. It looked to be made of luxurious wool, and inside it was lined with fleece. 'Put it on,' he said with impatience, 'before you turn into an ice block.'

'You bought me a coat?'

'And gloves, a hat and scarves,' he enumerated impatiently. 'While it would solve some problems

for me, I don't actually wish you to die of hypo-
thermia.'

She glared at him. He could be such a bastard
sometimes! Sometimes? Try all the time. Default
setting: rude.

'Gee, thanks,' she said, making it obvious she
wasn't at all grateful. Even though the moment she
slipped out of her old coat and into the new one,
her body temperature raised by several degrees.

She buttoned it up all the way and when she
lifted her gaze to his face she saw his attention
was fixated on the buttons. Particularly the ones at
chest height. He looked at her in a way that made
her pulse soar.

'Gloves,' he said thickly, turning away and
reaching into his car. The moment was over so
quickly that she almost wondered if it had happened at all, but the swirling of her blood was all
the confirmation she needed.

'But before you put them on—' he handed her
a small box '—start with this.'

It was said so unceremoniously that she had no
reason to suspect what she'd see when she lifted
the lid, so she did so without care.

But inside was a ring—an engagement ring, apparently. A huge green emerald was at the centre
and a circlet of white diamonds surrounded it, then
ran down either side and around the diameter. It
was beautiful, it was huge, it was *expensive*.

'Oh.' Abby blinked at the ring and then up at him. 'What is it?' she asked. Stupid question, but she was blindsided.

'What do you think?' He lifted it from the box and placed it in her palm. 'I hear they're part of the deal.'

'Deal?' She arched a brow.

'The getting married deal.'

Abby nodded, still not putting the ring on. 'But this is…too much. A simple band would have been fine, right?'

A muscle jerked in his jaw. 'A simple band is not the kind of ring I would buy for the woman I want to spend the rest of my life with. If we want people to believe this is a real marriage, then you'll have to convince them. Starting with the ring you wear.'

She frowned. 'Do we care what people think?'

A muscle throbbed in his jaw and his face was loaded with obvious derision. 'I care for our son's sake. I will not have him be subjected to gossip and cruelty because his parents cannot act like mature adults.' When she didn't react, he sighed heavily. 'Just put the ring on.'

She arched a brow. 'Gosh, seeing as you asked so nicely.' The words were uttered facetiously. Still, she didn't do as he said. Not to be ornery, but because she was truly miffed by the point he was making.

'Not for nothing, I don't think children get

teased for having unmarried parents in the twenty-first century.'

'We won't know for sure, will we, because Raf will have two parents who love him, and are apparently happy together.'

Abby looked down at the ring, her own green eyes reflected in the colour of the central gemstone. Her heart stuttered with the brief consideration that perhaps he'd chosen it for that reason. But it was absurd. He'd probably just picked the first ring he'd seen when he'd walked into the shop. That it happened to be this one was a coincidence.

'Are you having second thoughts about our arrangement?' he asked silkily. Her heart began to race. Internally, she rejected that very idea. She knew already that living here with Gabe was the right decision—the advantages to Raf were abundantly clear.

'No,' she said thoughtfully. 'But I think we should talk about what kind of marriage we're going to have.'

He looked as if he was about to say something—to argue with her—but then he angled his head. Was it a nod? An agreement?

'It makes sense,' she said firmly. And, knowing what would motivate Gabe, she pulled out the big guns. 'It's best for Raf.'

'Fine,' he said, retrieving a bag from the trunk and then closing it. 'Let's talk.' He spoke the word with obvious reluctance, as though it were the very last thing he wanted to do, yet at least he had conceded something.

He began to walk away from her and she followed with a frown, ring in one hand, shopping bag in the other. 'Gabe? Where are you going?'

He stopped walking, his expression frustrated. 'You wanted to talk?'

When she was close enough, he reached for her hand and unfurled her fingers, then slid the ring into place. His nod of approval showed that he, at least, was happy with the way it looked, even though it felt curiously heavy to Abby.

'There is a *caffè* around the corner.'

'Oh.' She nodded, for some reason having thought they would simply speak in the car on the return trip.

'I'm hungry,' he said, as if that explained his choice.

He held the door to the *caffè* open for her, and it took Abby a moment to see past her distracted thoughts and appreciate the beauty of the place. It was charming, only ten or so seats at a few tables, with bay windows that looked out onto the ancient street. Festivity was in abundance here. A tree was set up at one end of the room and it had been decorated with burgundy ribbons and gold tinsel. A small train ran in circles around its base. Carols played overhead, Italian words set to familiar tunes, so that Abby's mind hummed along even when her heart was cold.

'Have a seat,' he prompted, pointing to a table in the corner.

Abby shot him a look that straddled amusement and irritation. 'Would it kill you to *not* boss me around?'

He lifted a single dark brow. 'Probably.'

She fought the temptation to poke her tongue out and made her way to the table, sitting down at it heavily. Even the beautiful decorations she held couldn't cheer her up. She resisted an impulse to pull them from their packaging and look at them. That would be her special reward when she got back to the castle.

She turned towards Gabe unwillingly, noting the deference with which he was treated by the couple behind the counter. They seemed completely inspired by him, nodding as he gestured to various foods, speaking in rapid-fire Italian.

He was such a native of these parts, and yet she knew he'd spent a large part of his life in Australia. He spoke English like it wasn't his first language, still shying away from easy contractions and idioms.

He turned towards Abby unexpectedly. Their eyes locked and her pulse began to hammer hard inside her veins. She looked away, focusing her attention on a little scratch in the table top as though it were the most fascinating detail she'd ever observed.

'You wanted to talk,' he said, taking the seat opposite her. 'So?'

'Well...' She bit down on her lip, forcing her thoughts into order. 'Our marriage... I mean, you want people to think it's a real marriage, but...'

'Yes?' he prompted, his expression droll.

'It won't be.'

'No.'

She should have felt relieved by his rapid agreement, but she didn't. Something strange twisted inside her. 'So you don't...expect us to...'

'Sleep together?' he mocked, putting her out of her misery.

'Right.' She nodded jerkily. The woman from behind the counter appeared, placing two short black coffees down onto the table before swiftly disappearing.

Abby cupped one of the small glasses, simply to have something to do with her hands. It was warm and strangely comforting.

'As I said last night, sleeping together isn't on the agenda.' The words were so cold that Abby couldn't doubt their truth. 'My preference would have been never to see you again, after that night. As you know.' He paused for a moment. 'But I'm prepared to put that aside for our son. I truly believe this is the right decision.'

Abby nodded, though she could no longer separate sense from stupidity. A thousand and one questions raced through her mind. If they weren't sleeping together, would he sleep with someone else? Would her life include putting up with a series of Gabe's mistresses? What if he fell in love with one of them? What if he wanted to *marry* one of them? And they sued her for custody of Raf and won?

Suddenly her heart was thumping too hard, too fast, and she knew she had to fight her natural reserve to do what was best not just for Raf but also for herself.

'But there'll be no one else,' she said, her chin tilted forward defiantly.

His smile was smug and condescending. 'Does the idea make you jealous?'

'No,' she said. 'You're the one who's worried about exposing Raf to gossip. Don't you think extramarital affairs might qualify?'

He eyed her thoughtfully. 'I have every intention of doing what is right for our son, at every step of the way.'

It was strangely worded and yet his statement reassured Abby. It hadn't been a promise, yet she trusted him. She believed him.

Did that make her a fool?

'And for how long?'

He lifted a brow in silent enquiry.

'How long do you see this "marriage" of ours lasting?'

'As long as he needs us,' Gabe said, and something in the words pierced Abby's heart. 'At some point in the future we will separate. When he is older, when he's happy and settled. It's impossible to say now when that time will come.'

Abby nodded, wondering why his words didn't offer more relief.

'Rest assured, *tempesta*, I will not keep you at my side longer than is necessary.'

He threw his coffee back, oblivious to the way Abby's face went ashen at his throwaway sentence. She hid her reaction quickly, grateful when a waitress appeared with food. There were *piadini* and *zeppole*, *biscotti* and fruit. He hadn't been kidding about being hungry—he'd ordered enough to feed a family of five.

But her appetite had diminished; his final statement had left Abby with a sinking feeling deep in her gut. He hated her, he hated that they were marrying, yet he was prosaically willing to accept it— but only for so long as was absolutely necessary.

'How long did you study dancing?' he asked, changing the subject neatly.

Her ballet career was a subject she generally took great care to avoid. But with Gabe Arantini? She was emotionally disorientated.

'A while.'

'A year? Two? Five?'

'Does it matter?'

He leaned closer and surprised her by putting his hand on hers, his fingers grazing over the top of the engagement ring. 'We are going to need to get better at pretending we don't dislike one another,' he said softly. 'It is natural that I should know this about you. So?'

He was right, and that annoyed her. 'Eleven years,' she said quietly. And then, surprising herself, she continued to speak, her eyes trained on the table top, her lips moving without her consent. 'My mother was a prima ballerina, so beautiful and graceful. I wanted to be just like her.'

He nodded. 'How old were you when she died?'

She'd mentioned this on their first night together, though she'd been careful to omit any details that might give away her identity.

'I was eight,' she murmured, the memories heavy on the periphery of her mind. 'It was a month before Christmas. A traffic accident. Very unexpected.'

'I'm sorry.' His civility surprised her.

'And you began to learn ballet after she died?'

She nodded. 'My father knew I wanted to be like Mom. But it was more than that. *He* wanted me to be like her. I look like her,' she said quietly. 'And I move like her.' That was a lie. Abby had been told several times by careless, callous people that her mother's talent had been *nothing* to Abby's. As though that were praise and not a dagger through a grieving daughter's heart.

'What happened?' he asked, shifting a little in his seat.

'It was a child's dream,' she said, ignoring the lurch of pain in her chest.

'You grew out of the dream?'

That wasn't precisely true. And, though she generally didn't speak about her ballet career, she felt compelled to make Gabe understand, to explain the truth. 'It's a funny thing, being good at something.' Her smile was just a ghost. 'I *was* good at ballet, Gabe. Very good. Exceptionally good.' She spoke without even a hint of bragging. She was simply admitting the truth. 'I was given amazing opportunities. I danced with some of the world's best.'

'And then?' he prompted when she took a pause to bite into a strawberry.

'I broke my leg,' she said, a smile curving her lips at the reminiscence.

He waited for her to continue.

'And I could no longer rehearse. I had to rest. For the first time in my life, I had time to explore new diversions, and I discovered, much to everyone's displeasure, that there were things I loved more than dancing.'

He nodded thoughtfully. 'So you quit?'

'Yes.' She nodded slowly. 'A friend brought me

Jane Eyre one evening. It was supposed to be a joke. He teased me that I was a bit like Bertha in the attic, and I wouldn't understand until I'd read the book.'

She laughed.

'It was silly—he was playing on the fact that I was "locked up" by Dad, but of course that wasn't true. Anyway, by the time I finished it I was hooked, and I devoured anything I could get my hands on. I realised there was so much more to life than dancing. Books, for one thing. I wanted to read everything ever written.'

Abby fingered one of the cinnamon doughnuts, her mind far away.

'I just… I didn't want my whole life to be consumed by ballet any more. My every waking thought given over to the act of dance. Oh, no. I wanted to be in the ocean, aboard the *Pequod*, or in ancient Troy by Agamemnon's side as he fought Achilles, I wanted to be at Manderley and Thornfield Hall, I wanted to be twenty thousand leagues under the sea. I thought breaking my leg and missing rehearsals for so many months was an ending, but it was a beginning. The world opened up to me in a way I had never even hoped it would.'

Gabe's lips were tight. 'Yet you still dance?'

'Oh, I'll always dance,' she agreed. 'I love it as a hobby, but I don't want to spend my life pursuing it as a career.'

'You said your father wanted you to be like your mother. How did he take your decision to abandon professional ballet?'

Abby dropped her head forward, not wanting to answer. Her father had behaved appallingly; it was impossible to convey that to Gabe without allowing him to condemn her father, and it wasn't that simple.

'He got over it,' she said stiffly.

'I'll bet he didn't.' Gabe eyes narrowed. 'Yet you still adore him enough to do his bidding?'

She swallowed. How could she explain that, in part, guilt at disappointing her father had motivated many of her decisions, including the one that had brought her to Gabe's feet? A desperate, soul-deep need to impress a man who was, perhaps, impossible to impress?

'He's my father.' She shrugged. 'It's hard to explain. I know he has his faults,' she whispered. 'But I love him.'

'And you'd forgive him anything?'

'I guess,' she said, bright green eyes meeting his glittering black. 'Wouldn't you do the same?'

Gabe's laugh was a scoff. 'No, *tempesta*. I destroyed my father at the first opportunity I had and I would do the same a hundred times over.'

CHAPTER EIGHT

ABBY STARED AT RAF, a frown etched on her face. In the two weeks since the morning in Fiamatina, she'd barely spoken to Gabe, yet his statement had continued to play on her mind, making her wonder to the point of distraction.

He'd destroyed his father?

She thought of what she knew of the man who was to become her husband. He'd been raised by foster parents in Australia. That was how he'd met his business partner, she knew, because he'd mentioned it in passing only a week or so earlier, as though it hardly mattered. He'd gone into the foster system at eight—she'd remembered because it was the same age her own life had been turned on its head when her mother had died.

But before that?

She had no idea, and now she *wanted* to know.

She could ask him, but Gabe hadn't seemed at all forthcoming after he'd dropped the bombshell. He'd skated around the topic, talking instead about logistics for the wedding—the licences that would be necessary, given that she was American. It could take time, he'd warned.

That was fine with Abby. It wasn't that she regretted having agreed to marry him, but a little time to adjust to her new circumstances would be good.

Necessary.

Essential.

Only she'd barely seen him for two weeks and she was beginning to suspect that he was avoiding her.

Fighting an urge to reach down and cuddle Raf, she slipped out of his room, making her way to her own bedroom. She didn't think of Gabe as she passed his door; it was too dangerous.

From her room, she spied the forest that surrounded the castle and suddenly she remembered the idea that had occurred to her weeks earlier in Fiamatina. Perhaps the conversation with Gabe had pushed all else from her mind, because she'd barely thought of the delightful Christmas decorations either. They were still sitting in the shopping bag. She pulled them out now, setting them on her dressing table with reverence, smiling as she observed how beautiful and special they were. And they would look even better on a tree!

Surely they deserved a tree?

With renewed determination, she grabbed the coat Gabe had given her—several more had been added to her wardrobe since then, arriving in boxes from Milan, Venice, Paris and Prague. It was a thoughtful gesture but Abby resented feeling like a beneficiary of his patronage.

She'd come to know many of the household staff well, including Hughie, a young Irishman who'd taken over much of the work in the grounds around the castle. It was Hughie who cleared the snow several times a day. She liked him best, perhaps because he spoke English and so they were able to converse easily. He also had a soft spot for Raf, which was instantly endearing.

'Hughie?' She found him bent over the fireplace, stocking it with fresh wood.

He lifted his head and grinned, a smile that would bring most women to their knees. Unfortunately for Abby, only one smile in the world had the ability to set her pulse racing and she had to rely on her memories of it. She hadn't seen a lot of Gabe's smile since she'd come to Italy.

'Do you think you could help me with something?'

'Anything.' He stood up and wiped his hands on the worn fronts of his jeans. 'You look like you've got mischief on your mind,' he said, wiggling his brows.

'Definitely,' Abby laughed. 'I want to put up a tree.'

'A Christmas tree?'

'Yep. No shortage of trees to choose from, right? But I don't have an axe. Or experience with felling trees, come to think of it. And I thought...'

'Oh, yeah, sure.' Hughie grinned. 'I'll bring one

down for you right now, before the dark settles. Come on. You can even pick it.'

It was the first real fun Abby had had in a long time. They walked through the dense woods for half an hour, talking about Hughie's family back home—six sisters and parents who adored their brood—which made Abby incredibly jealous.

He was moving onto describing his oldest sister, Daphne, when Abby froze.

'It's *perfect*,' she squealed, jumping up and down on the spot.

'Sheesh!' Hughie grinned. 'You couldn't 'ave chosen a tree closer to the castle, huh?'

'Sorry…' She winced. 'Can we have this one?'

'Yeah, I reckon we can.' He lifted the chainsaw. 'Stand back, then.'

She did, watching with admiration as he chainsawed through most of the thick trunk and then gave it a kick, felling the tree easily.

Once it was down, Hughie rigged a rope around the tree's base and then began to drag it through the soft snow.

'Won't that break the branches?' she asked. 'It'd be a shame to get it back to the house and find it's only half-perfect.'

'You'd just have to display it facing outwards,' he teased. 'Nah, it's soft needles, see.' He stopped walking so she could feel them. He was right; they were luxuriant beneath her touch. 'They'll be fine.'

They walked towards the house and Abby was so relieved to simply be having a normal conversation with someone that all of her attention was focused on Hughie. She didn't see Gabe glowering down at them from one of the upstairs windows. If she'd looked up, she would have seen his expression was one of utter fury.

He had forgotten how beautiful she was. No, that wasn't true. He'd remembered her beauty, but he had trained himself to look beyond it, to remember that her heart was quick to manipulate and lie. Every time he saw her smile and wanted to smile back, he remembered the photographs on her phone. The pictures of the Calypso design files that she'd snapped to show to her father—to bring his company down. It was easy to harden himself to her charms in the face of such obvious duplicity.

Every time she hummed under her breath and the song wound around his chest, tying him up in Abigail knots, he reminded himself that he'd had every reason to walk away from her and refuse to see her again.

When he woke up in the middle of the night in a cold sweat at dreaming of her pregnant and alone, wishing he could reach out and touch her, comfort her, know her, he reminded himself that *her* lies, *her* deceit had made that impossible.

He'd taught himself to ignore her beauty.

Only watching Abby as she was now, laughing with Hughie, he couldn't help but notice. Her smile, her dimples, her sparkling eyes, the grace and fluidity of movement that were as much a part of her as were her arms and legs.

He'd kept her at a distance this last fortnight, and he'd been glad. As if every day that passed without more than an occasional civility, a brief greeting, proved that he was up to the challenge of being married to Abigail and not capitalising on the chemistry that flashed between them.

Hughie's face was animated. He said something low and Abby had to lean closer to hear it properly. Her body, wrapped in one of the coats he'd bought her, made Gabe's pulse throb. She tucked her hair behind her ear, her expression serious as she concentrated on what Hughie said, and then she laughed again, reaching a hand out and touching his forearm. Their eyes met and Hughie's look of admiration was obvious.

Gabe swore into his office and dragged a hand through his hair.

She was serious now, her expression almost haunted, her eyes focused on the house, and Gabe's heart shifted in his chest. She was beautiful when she laughed, and enigmatic when she was sombre. Both emotions seemed to call to him in a way he utterly resented.

Just the sight of another man looking at Abby

like Hughie was stirred a dark, possessive lust within Gabe's bones.

She was the mother of his child, the woman who'd given her virginity to him. She was *his* in so many ways… He just had to remind her of that.

'Where do you want it?' Hughie asked, straightening the tree as though it were simply a bunch of flowers.

'I suppose the study?' Abby murmured, thinking of the room that had the comfortable leather lounges and a view of the alps.

'The study is nice,' Hughie said. 'But it's out of the way, and I'm not sure this beast you've chosen will fit. It might have to be the entrance hall.'

He was right. Here at the house, without the other enormous trees dwarfing it, Abby could see the tree she'd chosen was actually quite large.

'Okay.' She nodded in agreement, equally pleased with the idea of the tree being set in the midst of the beautiful armchairs and sofa that sat in the foyer.

'Abigail?' There was a coldness in Gabe's voice. She turned to face him slowly, marshalling her expression into one of dispassionate curiosity, ignoring the kaleidoscope of butterflies that had begun to beat against her insides.

Why did he have to be so handsome? Even now,

wearing dark jeans and a black pullover, he looked like a piece of art.

'I need you for a moment.'

'Oh.' Abby chewed on her lip. 'We were just about to set up the tree...'

'I can see that,' Gabe responded with barely suppressed anger.

'You're all right, Abby,' Hughie interrupted with a grin. 'I can wrangle this monster on my own.'

She was sure he could, but that wasn't the point. She'd been looking forward to helping. She shot Gabe a look of impatience but when she saw the dark, almost tortured emotions in the lines around his eyes, her own emotions ebbed. Had something serious happened?

'Okay.' She had a sense of urgency about her now. 'I'll be back soon.'

When she was level with Gabe on the stairs, he began to move upwards and she did her utmost to remain as far away from him as possible.

When they reached the landing though, he put a hand in the small of her back and steered her down the hallway at speed.

'I can walk just fine by myself, thank you,' she said tersely.

He threw her a fulminating glare.

'What the heck is going on?' she asked, coming to a stop halfway down the corridor.

'I would prefer to discuss it in private.' He nodded pointedly towards a door and, curiosity growing, she went with him.

'Fine, we're in private now,' she said once they were ensconced in her bedroom. She determinedly tried to ignore the presence of the bed.

Gabe shut the door.

'You tell me you're worried about rumours of infidelity, but at the first chance you get you're out there flaunting yourself for all the world to see.'

Abby froze. 'What?'

'You were practically fawning over Hughie just now.'

She gaped, speechless, lost for words.

He prowled towards her. 'You actually think sleeping with a member of our household staff is appropriate?'

'He's not "our" household staff, he's yours,' she snapped.

'An unimportant distinction.'

'And I'm *not* sleeping with him,' she denied hotly. 'I like him, okay? He's nice to me and we speak the same language. He's the only other person I've actually been able to talk to since I moved to Italy. He's *nice* to me, unlike a certain other someone I could mention and, newsflash, Gabe, it's refreshing to spend time with someone who doesn't look at me like I'm dirt on the sole of their shoe.'

He glared at her, his expression darker, if possible. 'I don't care that he's *nice* to you,' Gabe snapped. 'He's off-limits. I don't want to see you talking to him again.'

She made a scoffing sound. 'You can't click your fingers and just *forbid* me from having a friend.'

'No? But I can fire him,' Gabe responded, taking another step towards her, his expression mutinous.

'Don't you dare.' Abby pushed at his chest but he caught her hands, holding them in place, and when her eyes met his now, sparks of another variety flew, like their own localised fireworks display, erupting between their chests.

'Don't you tell me what I can and can't do. I'm not going to have you carrying on with whoever you decide you want…'

'Oh, grow up,' she said, pushing at his chest again. He pulled her hands down, holding them by her side, his breath heavy. 'I'm not sleeping with your gardener. I'm not sleeping with anyone! I haven't slept with anyone since you, so you can just go to hell with all your stupid accusations.'

Gabe's expression shifted momentarily and then it was fiercely intense and, before Abby knew what was happening, he was kissing her.

No, it wasn't a kiss, it was so much more. It was a mark of utter, unquestionable possession. It was a raging, desperate connection. His lips mashed to hers, his tongue slid inside her mouth and she made a noise of surprise and then surrender, low in her throat, her hands pulling free of his grip and reaching under his shirt, connecting with his bare chest, skin she remembered so intimately.

It had been over a year since they'd done this and yet it felt as if no time had passed. Or was it that they—this—existed outside the bounds of time and space?

'You won't be with anyone else,' he grunted, ripping his shirt over his head so she could marvel at his naked chest. He crushed her to him, kissing her desperately once more, his hands lifting to her hair and tangling in its length. It was still cold from her time in the snow and perhaps that reminded him of what they'd been fighting about, because he made another darkly guttural noise before stepping out of his trousers and pants so that he was completely naked.

'You are mine,' he said, pushing her shirt off, his expression deadly serious.

'I'm *not* yours,' she snapped. 'How can I be? You don't even speak to me. You don't look at me. I'm not yours.'

'I'm looking at you now.' He pushed at her jeans at the same time she stepped out of them. She wasn't his, but she was sure as hell desperate for him.

There was a vital difference, she told herself.

'I don't want you to just look at me,' she said boldly.

His laugh was hoarse. 'That's just as well.'

He ran his hands over her back, his fingertips gliding trails of goosebumps over her skin.

'You are too beautiful for your own good,' he groaned. His mouth came down on her breast, taking a nipple deep in his mouth, rolling it with his tongue, teasing it between his teeth so that shards of pleasure and pain shot through her body like little lightning bolts. His fingers toyed with her other breast, his palm wrapping around her, holding her weight, his thumb and forefinger rubbing over her nipple until she was crying out, moaning his name over and over again.

'You want me?' he asked, something grim in the question.

'Yes.' She wasn't afraid to admit that; she was afraid of what would happen if she didn't. She was afraid of this coming to an end when she needed Gabe, in that moment, more than she'd ever needed anything from anyone.

'Good,' he growled. 'Because I intend to make your body so desperate for mine that you cannot go a day without feeling me inside of you.'

She gasped at the promise, excitement flooding her veins.

'I thought you didn't want to touch me.'

'Apparently, I was wrong,' he admitted, lifting

her up and wrapping her legs around his waist. His
arousal was so hard and so close to her that she
tried to push down, to take him deep inside her
but he made a tsking noise. 'Be patient, *tempesta*.'

He placed her on the bed, his kiss pushing her
back so that his weight was on top of her. He disappeared, but only for a moment, and when he returned it was with a foil square in his hands. He
sheathed himself and she held her breath, needing
so desperately to feel him.

'Is this what you want?' he asked, pressing his
arousal to her womanhood gently, teasing, so that
she nodded, her brow fevered, her eyes hungry.

'Say please,' he commanded.

'Please,' she whimpered, arching her back.

'Tell me again that I am the only man you've
slept with,' he demanded, pushing himself a little
deeper inside her, so that she groaned softly.

'Yes, yes.' She lifted her hands over her head.

He pulled out completely. 'Say it.'

Her eyes jerked open but she nodded. 'I haven't
been with anyone since you.'

His smile was grim but he gave her what she
needed, thrusting deeper into her feminine core.
Still not deep enough, but she let out a low, soft
moan as pleasure rippled through her.

Her fingernails dug deep into his back, scor-
ing his shoulders as she lifted her legs, needing
to wrap around his waist, to hold him closer, but

he caught her knees and held her apart, kept her at a distance, his control and mastery of her body absolute.

'Please,' she cried out, desperate for release, for pleasure, for Gabe.

He dropped his mouth to her breast and flicked her nipple with his tongue, then ran his mouth down her body, over her flat stomach, across the dip of her navel and the apex of her thighs.

She gasped when his mouth connected with her most intimate flesh. 'Has a man ever touched you here?'

She whimpered and shook her head, digging her fingernails into the bed sheets.

His tongue ran across her seam and perspiration dampened her brow, her nipples pushed hard into the air, her whole body covered in goosebumps.

'I've changed my mind,' he said against her, his fingers running over her hips, finding her thighs and spreading them, giving him greater access.

'What about?' The question was panted, the words husky.

'I want you in my bed every night. Like this. Begging for me.'

She arched her back, her brain unable to engage and function, her mind non-existent.

'I need you,' she cried out.

'Then say you agree,' he said, his tongue dipping inside her so that she lost the ability to speak as well as to think. She was incandescent with desire, so completely overcome by the consuming need of him, so fully in the moment that she couldn't respond at all.

He lifted away from her and she let out a guttural noise of impatience.

'This is torture,' she snapped, pushing up on her elbows, panting, her long hair across her face.

He nodded. 'Yes.' He brought his body back to hers, his weight pleasing, his absence from her body not. 'I will torture you until you admit to me what you want.'

'I have,' she groaned, wrapping her legs around his waist.

As with before, he pushed her knees downward, shaking his head. 'I'm not having a wife who runs around with a gardener, or anyone else. Not when we make such sense together in bed.'

Through the fog of sensual desire, the words pushed into her brain. He was acknowledging that this was special, different and addictive, for him as well.

'Well,' she said, the word husky, thick, angry. 'That goes both ways. I won't have a husband who runs around with *anyone*.'

His eyes sparkled with something like an acknowledgement and he nodded, bringing his hard, firm arousal back to her feminine core. 'Deal,' he said, sliding inside her, thrusting hard, so that she let out a cry of relief when he finally took possession of her, his body everything she remembered and so much more.

His fingers laced through hers, pushing them above her head, and he kissed her, his possession absolute. He stoked flames in her she hadn't known existent, his body was, in that instant, her reason for being. Every movement, every thrust, every touch, every kiss, sent her closer and closer towards the edge of sanity until she was crying out, pleasure like a single point of bright light in her brain, blinding her utterly.

'Gabe.' She whispered his name and he broke the kiss to look at her. 'Is this normal?'

She had no experience outside of what they'd shared, but if sex was like this—enough to tear you apart at your cosmic core—then how did people ever get anything done?

In answer, he pulled out of her, something like iron in his expression, his desertion intense, but then he thrust into her anew so that she bucked her hips hard, meeting his demands—more than meeting them, conquering them.

'No, *tempesta*.' The admission seemed ripped from the depths of his being. 'Nothing about this is normal.'

Among the desire, the longing, the pleasure and the delicious, sensual heat, Abby knew she felt relief at that. She was glad this was different, even for him. She wanted to ask more, to ask him if he'd ever felt this, if he'd felt this the first time they were together, if he could tell her why it was so incredible between them.

But then he kissed her again and she surrendered to the moment completely, lost to the pleasure of their connection and the power of his body.

Pleasure began to spin in her gut, slow and insistent, before bursting through her whole body, promising delight and release, and she called his name over and over, arching her back, welcoming his every movement, taking him in deep, kissing him as though her life depended on it.

His hands sought her breasts, palming them, moving over them, and her release didn't abate, she was building anew, wave after wave of pleasure dousing her until she almost couldn't bear it.

At the moment she began to fall apart, he joined her, swearing under his breath as he thrust into her so deep and hard that it tipped her completely over the edge. She wasn't conscious of how loud she was being until he laughed, a choked sound, and pressed his lips to hers. Not a kiss of passion so much as to silence her.

Their breathing was in unison, just the inhalation and exhalation of two bodies that had been torn apart by sensual heat.

It had been the most intense pleasure of her life. Abby only realised now that he had been gentle with her in New York. That he had taken her innocence slowly, softly, subjugating his own desires to meet her own, initiating her into the way of lovemaking and desire in a way that would enable her to feel maximum pleasure.

But now?

No-holds-barred sex, and it had rocked her world to the core.

'That was amazing,' she sighed.

His body was still heavy on hers, his breathing deep, and she wondered if he'd fallen asleep until he shifted and his eyes met hers. 'You are mine,' he said darkly, seriously, reminding her of the argument they'd had before they'd slept together. 'I do not want to see you talking to Hughie again, as though he is your lover...'

'Gabe—' Abby smiled, trying to hold onto the threads of what they'd just shared, needing to be enveloped by intimacy for a little longer '—how can you think about anyone else after that? How can you think I am?'

'You forget, Abigail, that I know what you're capable of. That I have no reason to think the best of you.'

And the desire that had made her body so warm gave way to ice-cold regret. Remorse.

She pulled away from him, pushing him off her at the same time she jack-knifed off the bed, her face pale, her expression mutinous.

'How dare you throw insults at me after what we just shared?' she demanded through teeth that were chattering.

'We just shared sex,' he said with a nonchalant shrug. 'Albeit fantastic sex, but it doesn't change who you are.'

Abby shifted away from him, her eyes seeking her clothes, needing, desperately, to shield herself from him. 'You don't know anything about me,' she said, finding her underpants first and sliding them up her shaking legs, grateful for the modesty they afforded.

His short, sharp laugh was a dismissal that twisted her heart painfully in her chest. 'I know *everything* I need to know,' he corrected.

'Oh? Enlighten me,' she demanded, finding her jeans and turning them so they were the right side out.

'I don't need to enlighten you. You're not stupid.'

'Oh, I'm so glad that's not something you can fault me for.'

Gabe frowned, his expression one of true bemusement. 'After the way we met, I cannot change how I feel about you, nor what I think you are. But this—' he gestured to the bed '—this is a silver lining.'

'God—' she reached for her jumper, holding it in the palm of her hand '—you're such a bastard! You're cold and ruthless and heartless and so, so cruel. How can you think this marriage will ever work when you speak to me like that?'

'Have I said anything that's not true?'

'You don't know me,' she said, frustrated. 'You don't even try to know me!'

'You conned me into bed. Took photos of highly guarded, top-secret blueprints. You planned to pass them off to my competition…'

'I know all that,' she said on a small sob. 'But if you took a second to understand my relationship with my dad…'

'We all have a history.' Determination fired his veins. 'We all have baggage. You allowed yours to control you.'

He was right and she knew it. That angered her even further. She ripped the jumper through the air, shaking it pre-emptively and pulling it on, so she didn't see the way his face shifted, the way guilt momentarily glanced across his features. Regret too. The way he looked as if he hated that they were arguing and wasn't sure how to defuse it—to wind back his careless remark so that they were still entwined. Two bodies post-passion.

The sleeve of the jumper flew wide and as Abby jerked it over her head she heard a delicate, unmistakable breaking noise that mirrored the breaking of her heart.

'Oh, no!' For she knew immediately what had happened.

She spun around and, sure enough, one of the decorations had crashed to the ground, the other balancing precariously. She pushed it back to safety and then fell to her knees, her fingertips reaching for the tiny, fragile shards.

'Stop it.' Gabe swore, jumping from the bed and crouching beside her. But Abby didn't hear him. She blinked back tears that threatened to fall.

'Now look what you made me do,' she snapped, but the words lacked conviction.

'What is it?' He batted her hands away as she tried to pick up the pieces but she refused to comply, her fingertips seeking each shard as though she could somehow put them back together again.

'Stop,' he said softly, urgently. 'You're going to hurt yourself.'

Just as he said it, a piece of glass punctured her skin and a perfect droplet of crimson blood fell to the floor.

'Damn it.' He gripped her wrists and pulled her to standing. 'Sit here.'

He arranged her on the edge of the bed and disappeared into her bathroom. He returned with a wad of tissues, handing them to her. 'Press them to your skin.'

She pulled a face at his retreating back, refusing to watch while he cleaned up the vandalism of the perfect little decoration.

Only once the floor was clear of glass, the tiny

bell resting on the edge of the dressing table, did he come back to Abby. He crouched down in front of her, his eyes holding hers.

'What was that?'

She sniffed, refusing to meet his eyes.

'Abby?'

His use of the diminutive form of her name did something to her and she flicked her gaze to his, her own vulnerabilities unconsciously displayed in the lines of her beautiful young face. 'Christmas decorations,' she said softly. 'They were perfect.'

He looked towards the dressing table. 'Where did you get them?'

'A shop in Fiamatina,' she hiccoughed.

'So?' It was obvious he didn't comprehend. 'You can buy another one, *tempesta.*'

'No, I can't,' she sobbed, shaking her head then dropping it into her palms.

'Why not? Were there only two in the whole shop?'

'No, there were quite a few but...' She clamped her lips together, sucking in a deep breath.

'But?' he prompted.

'They were expensive, okay? I could only afford two. And I loved them. They were special and rare and I was going to put them on the Christmas tree for Raf's first Christmas and every Christmas after and now it's all ruined. Everything is ruined.'

CHAPTER NINE

GABE WATCHED THEM from his office, every cell held taut. They hadn't spoken again since he'd left her room the day before. Her anger had been disproportionate to the perceived crime. No, not crime. It hadn't been his fault. She'd knocked the decoration herself, and yet she'd blamed him. She'd been so cross with him—he hadn't known her capable of that anger.

When they'd argued in New York, she'd been passive. She'd taken his remonstration, she'd accepted what he'd laid at her feet and she'd been sad, apologetic. She had known how wrong she'd been. Yes, he had seen shame in her eyes—remorse too—and she'd been reasonable enough not to argue in the face of his anger.

Yesterday, *she'd* been enraged.

And not about the decoration. Not really. It was more than that. The way he'd treated her, the things he'd said.

Regret perforated the lining of his gut.

He'd been shocked by his weakness—shocked by his very emotional response to seeing her with Hughie. It had been an innocent conversation and he'd acted as though he'd caught them *in flagrante*. He'd taken her into her bedroom, knowing that if they didn't have sex he'd be driven almost insane by possessive need.

And then he'd done what he could to turn back time, to remind them both of why they were enemies more than lovers.

An unfamiliar sense of shame flooded him. He hadn't enjoyed hurting her. He hadn't liked seeing her shock, feeling her withdraw from him, physically needing to distance herself from him.

He closed his eyes, flashes of their time together running before him. Her passion— a passion that had been unmatched in his experience—the way she'd given herself to him completely. What cruel twist of fate was it that a woman he despised had turned out to be his perfect partner in bed? More than that, she was the mother of his child and he was committed to spending his life with her, to making their child happy.

He couldn't do that if he spent the whole time berating her for the sins in her past, yet he couldn't move beyond those sins until he understood her better. He had every reason to be careful with his trust—his childhood had been a baptism of fire and he'd developed the necessary defences. That included being careful who he admitted to his inner sanctum—which so far just included Noah.

Now, there was also Raf.

He opened his eyes and his gaze instantly pinpointed Abby, a bright shape against the white backdrop of snow. He studied her. She was smiling and despite the fact their child, so bundled up he was three times his usual size, couldn't possibly comprehend her, she was talking as she built an enormous snowman. His cheeks were ruddy from where he sat propped in a stroller.

Gabe watched as Abby pinched a small amount of snow in her fingertips and pressed a tiny bit to Raf's cheek. Their baby's eyes flew wide and then the little boy smiled. She smiled back. Something within Gabe squeezed. What must it be like to have that kind of affection?

Maternal love was a foreign concept to him.

Any love, really.

Abby had it to give in spades, apparently.

She turned back to the snowman and kept building, fattening his belly until her arms couldn't wrap around him. Some time later, when she was happy with the construction, she reached into the bottom of the stroller and pulled out something red and white. A scarf! She wrapped it around the snowman's neck and tied it in a knot, then she reached for something else. A Santa hat.

She was making a damned Santa snowman on his lawn, with their son. Was this what it would always be like for him? On the periphery of something—a family—and not being able to reach for it? Was this the lasting legacy of his own childhood?

He didn't believe in love—even as a boy, witnessing the way love had slowly deadened his mother's soul, he swore he'd never get married, never have children. He hadn't wanted either. The necessity of loving wasn't something he'd ever craved.

Did that excuse his behaviour?

Did anything?

Making sure Abby married him was one thing; using her innocence and desire against her to keep her in his bed was another. He had kissed her and she'd quivered. She'd said she hadn't been with anyone else and he believed her. It wasn't as if she'd had a multitude of opportunities since she'd been so sick while carrying his baby. But if he hadn't brought her to Italy? No doubt she would have found someone to share her life with.

The very idea filled Gabe's mouth with acidity.

In bed she was putty in his hands and there was so much he could teach her, so much he could do to help her forget how imperfect their situation was. Keeping her in a sensual fog so that she never stopped to question the madness of what they were doing. Was he really capable of that? Could he stoop so low?

His expression was grim because, deep down, he knew that as long as she was under his roof, with his ring on her finger, he would do whatever it took to have her.

He would never love her—never trust her—and

nor would he ever forgive her; but he would make love to her often because they both wanted that. That was the only part of this whole plan that made sense—the rest was a minefield…

She laughed again with Raf, and certainty formed as a rock in his gut. *She was his.*

'I have to go to Rome.' His voice came from the door to her room and Abby paused her reading, pressing a finger against the page of her book and looking up in the hope it wasn't obvious what effect his appearance was having on her.

Had it only been a day ago that they'd made love? For confirmation, her eyes flew to the dressing table where a solitary ornament remained.

'Rome?' She sat up straighter in bed, her heart hammering against her ribcage. He was wearing a suit, just like the first night they'd met, and he looked so damned handsome it was impossible to remember that she was still frustrated with him. With great difficulty, she did, though.

Her voice was cool. 'Well, have fun.'

Gabe stepped into her room, closing the door behind him and striding across to the bed. Abby's pulse accelerated.

'I would have more fun here,' he admitted gruffly. His strong, confident hands caught her thighs and pulled her to the edge of the bed; Abby's breath caught in her throat and she stared up at him with such obvious passion that she knew he must see it, must comprehend.

'Do you remember what we discussed?' he asked, moving his head closer to hers so only an inch separated them.

She shook her head, merely because she couldn't think straight and needed to buy time.

He lifted a finger and pressed it to her cheek, then ran it down her jaw to her neck, and to the pulse point hovering at the base of her throat. 'You are mine,' he said simply.

She opened her mouth to argue, to say something to assert herself, but he took the opportunity to kiss her, his lips taking hers, pressing her back to the bed so that his body was on top of hers and she moaned into him, such a sweet sound of innocence that his gut twisted.

'I want you to share my room,' he murmured, the words seductive, as was the way he moved his kiss to her throat, nipping her with his teeth while his hands ran over her body, finding the flesh beneath her shirt. She wasn't wearing a bra; he was easily able to cup her breasts, to feel their warm sweetness, her tight nipples.

She made a noise of acquiescence, a garbled sound of pleasure.

'You'll move in with me,' he said, a little more confident now but still miles from his usual arrogance.

'I *have* moved in with you.' She said the words into his mouth, kissing him, her ache to be possessed by him profound.

'You know what I mean.'

He seemed to be asking, to *want* something from her without simply demanding it. She tilted her head to the side. 'I'll think about it.'

He lifted his head and his eyes glowed, but he wisely chose not to push the point.

Distance knifed between them and she wanted to bridge it, but he was already straightening, pulling further away from her.

'How long will you be gone?' She tried to make the question sound casual when in fact she was irrationally bothered by the idea of him so far away.

'A day or so.' He took a step back, his eyes holding hers, the rapid shift of his chest the only sign that he had been at all affected by the kiss they'd just shared.

'Be good while I'm gone. And, just to save you some time, there are *no* Calypso files in the castle, so you don't need to go looking behind my back.'

She glared at him but he shook his head.

'It was a joke. A bad one.' His smile was tight. 'I'll see you soon.'

It had been a joke but the words stung, in the way that only the truth could. When she looked back to that night in New York, she could scarcely believe what she'd done. It was as if someone else had temporarily taken over her body.

And now she'd have to face that misstep for the rest of her life. Or for as long as this charade of a marriage continued.

When he was out of sight she picked up her book and continued to read, but without seeing a single word. Less than an hour later, she heard the helicopter take off and moved—as if on autopilot—to the window. It was shiny black; it looked like a huge eagle, all sleek and elegant, as it moved away from her and the castle.

She told herself she was relieved he was gone, that it would give her time to make sense of what was happening between them. But, in truth, relief was nowhere near the top of what she felt.

She dropped her head to her pillow and breathed in deeply. It still smelled of him.

She groaned—she didn't have to analyse her feelings to know that she had them, and to know that it was inherently dangerous to feel *anything* for a man like Gabe Arantini. Particularly given that he had made it obvious he didn't like her and would never trust her.

And yet…

Yes—and yet. Apparently, her heart hadn't got her brain's memo, for it was already softening and turning, allowing Gabe more space inside her mind than she knew was wise.

Telling herself she was going to make the most of this opportunity to explore, she didn't want to acknowledge that she was actually marking time however she could.

She woke early the next morning and, wrapped up in her warmest clothes, went to explore the forest to the side of the house. She found pine cones which she could spray-paint silver and use to decorate the tree, and she counted seven squirrels as she went.

She imagined Raf when he was older. She imagined the way his face would light up at the sight of the bushy-tailed creatures, the way he'd laugh and try to chase them. Her chest heaved.

It was right that she was here in Italy, here with Gabe. She'd hated Gabe for sweeping into her life and expecting her to fall in with all these changes, but when she thought of the tiny apartment in Manhattan with no heating she knew their son would be happier here.

And her? She pushed that question aside.

Reliving the time they'd spent together in Manhattan, she played with Raf, noticing every little detail about him anew. She lay with him on his tummy, she read to him, she watched him sleep and she got to know the nannies who also looked after him.

Gabe had told Abby she wouldn't need to cook but to distract herself she dug out a recipe book from the castle's library and made gingerbread dough until the whole kitchen was fragrant with the spiced aroma. And though she'd never attempted anything so grand as a gingerbread house, she figured she was already way outside her comfort zone so what was one more brave attempt?

It was almost dark by the time she was finished, the house hardly a work of art but at least structurally sound. She went back upstairs but instead of returning to her bedroom, she went to his.

He'd asked her to move in. Was that what she wanted?

She padded into his suite, hovering on the threshold as though she were crossing some invisible barrier before pushing deeper inside. His room was larger than hers, with a king-size bed at its heart, two sofas to the side and a bay window that overlooked the gardens. She wondered what these gardens would be like in summer. It was hard to imagine while they were completely blanketed in snow.

There were no marks of personal possession in this room, besides his clothes in the wardrobe and toiletries in the en suite bathroom. No photos hung on the walls, no artwork to show his aesthetic preference. There was a flat-screen television mounted on the wall. She flicked it to life distractedly—the Italian news was on. She sat on the edge of the bed, watching for a while, wondering if she'd ever comprehend the fast-moving language.

Hours later, she accepted that Gabe wasn't coming back to the castle.

The wave of disappointment was unwelcome, but she recognised that feeling well.

She showered and dressed in a pair of wintry pyjamas before curling up in her own bed.

She fell asleep dreaming of Gabe and woke with a start some time in the middle of the night, sitting up straight. She was disorientated, as though she might have been in his room after all, as though he might be with her.

A cursory inspection with the light of her lamp showed that not to be the case. She was alone in her own bed.

She dropped back against the pillows and stared at the ceiling until the oblivion of dawn or sleep came first.

In the end, it was dawn. Morning light broke across her room and she was grateful, if somewhat exhausted, to step out of bed, shower and dress.

Her previous day's distractions had only worked so much.

She spent an hour with Raf and then pulled on some leggings and a form-fitting shirt and went to the room near the kitchen.

Ballet would help.

She chose a piece from *Les Petit Riens* to punish herself. The choreography included seven back-to-back *fouettes* then a double *pirouette* and she loved it for its intricacy. The hardest dances always looked the most beautiful, the most deceptively effortless, when they were performed well.

She breathed in deeply, her eyes closed as she felt the music, and then she began to move, her eyes remaining closed as she lost herself to the emotion of the Mozart piece, performing the *fouettes*—one of the most difficult steps in ballet—as though she were simply walking.

You're going to be a star, Abs. Just like your mom.

The words pushed against her and she frowned, slowing to a stop, dropping her head forward. Tears sparkled in her eyes when she thought of her father, when she thought of the fact that he was alone in America, that he was such a stubborn ass he'd let her go. No, he hadn't let her go. He'd pushed her—hard—out of his life.

She made a grunting noise, forcibly removing such thoughts, and continued to dance, pushing herself harder and harder, performing a *grande jeté* high in the air before landing gracefully on her feet and pushing up *en pointe*.

Had she known he was watching?

No.

Yet the sight of Gabe, draped against the door, as he had been the first time she'd practised in here, didn't surprise her. Their eyes met and everything inside her coiled tight like a spring. She was very still as the music swirled around them, enveloping them, throbbing with tension.

'Don't stop.' The words were more than a gravelly command. They were a hoarse, desperate plea.

She didn't like the way he told her what to do—her cheeks flushed because deep down she liked it very much—but she wanted to show her free will as much as possible. She felt his desperation, the lure of his need, and turned back to the dance, once again feeling it as though it were a part of her.

She didn't close her eyes though. If he wanted to watch her, then she wanted to watch him, to see the play of emotions on his face as she pirouetted around the room. For a moment she remembered what it had been like to perform, wearing the beautiful yet hard and scratchy costumes, the feet that had ached, the rapturous attention of the audience, the adoration from the other dancers. Though she'd come up against some jealousy, Abby moved so beautifully, so instinctively, that most ballerinas had simply accepted she was different to the rest of them.

After half an hour the piece came to a stop and Abby paused with it, remembering the last movement of choreography as though she'd learned it only the day before. The *attitude derrière* was the final step and she held it long after the last note had throbbed around them, her eyes meeting

Gabe's, locking to his, before she eased her foot down and returned to standing.

She waited, her breath held, uncertain what he would say, only feeling that something powerful had shifted between them, something new and interesting.

'You…' He frowned, the words apparently stuck deep inside him. His voice was hoarse and she was glad because she knew it was emotion that did that. He had watched her and he'd *felt* something. That was the point of ballet, wasn't it? 'That was incredible.'

The praise, though not the most lavish she'd ever received, made her heart soar because praise wasn't something Gabe Arantini offered often.

'Thank you,' she said, even more pleased when she sounded calm in the face of her racing heart. 'How was Rome?'

He dipped his head forward and she had no idea what the gesture was supposed to convey.

'How is Raf?'

She smiled; she couldn't help it. 'Delightful.'

He arched a brow. 'You seem well. Less tired.'

'Well, having round-the-clock nanny care will do that for a mom,' she pointed out.

He nodded. 'I think he is settled here too.'

'Well, it's only been a few weeks. But yes. He seems to be settling in well.'

He frowned, and she had the sense that he was

trying to find words, that he was looking for what to say. But he didn't speak, and so Abby did. 'I... guess I'll go take a shower.'

He nodded but when she was almost at the door he reached out, wrapping his fingers around her wrist. 'Did you sleep in my bed?'

She blinked, the question unexpected. 'No.'

He made a small tsking noise. 'And here I was, imagining you there.'

She swallowed. 'It felt weird.'

He scanned her face intently and then nodded. 'No matter. There is tonight.'

Her stomach rolled with anticipation.

'I have to catch up on some work. Have lunch with me later? There's something I need to discuss with you.'

If she'd been planning on refusing, the last short sentence scuppered that intention. Curiosity fanned in her chest. 'Okay.'

She took a step towards the door but, instead of letting her go, he pulled her back to his body, firm, and she felt then that he was so hard, all of him, and she groaned softly under her breath.

'Did you miss me?' he asked softly, lifting his hand to her hair and tangling his fingers in its length.

'You were only gone for a night,' she pointed out.

'Was I? It felt like longer.'

CHAPTER TEN

THE BUTTERFLIES IN her stomach were rampant, swishing their delicate wings against her sides, making it difficult to concentrate on anything. She barely noticed the beautiful table she was led to, in a part of the castle she was yet to explore. A balcony beyond would be beautiful in warmer weather, but for now it remained sealed off, thick glass doors keeping the cold out but allowing an unimpeded view of the alpine scenery. A light dusting of snow had begun to fall and some of it settled on the railing as she watched. The table was round, large enough to comfortably accommodate six, but only two place-settings had been laid, and with the kind of cutlery and glassware one would find in a six-star restaurant.

She sucked in a deep breath, telling herself it was ridiculous to be nervous. The engagement ring Gabe had given her sparkled on her finger and Abby tried to draw strength from the beauty of its design—and failed. It was so lovely and perfect that it only added to her nervousness.

The domestic who'd shown her to the table had poured a glass of wine and Abby took a sip now, grateful to have something to occupy her hands. The alcohol was cold and yet warmed her insides. She closed her eyes and drew in another deep breath; when she blinked them open Gabe was striding into the room, a large black shopping bag held in one hand, so handsome that her breath snagged in her throat.

'I was held up,' he said by way of explanation rather than apology.

A wry smile touched Abby's lips.

'It's fine. I've only been here a few minutes.'

He nodded, taking the seat opposite her. Out of nowhere another domestic appeared, pouring Gabe some wine. He looked at the man with a frown. 'We can manage. I'd prefer not to be interrupted.'

The man said something in Italian, smiled at Abby and then disappeared.

Abby's frown was instinctive. 'You don't strike me as a man who would like having staff.'

He lifted a brow. 'Forty thousand people work for me.'

'I don't mean in a professional sense,' she said with a small shake of her head. 'I mean household staff.'

'You get used to it.' He shrugged.

'I don't know if I ever could.'

'You mean, if you ever *will*,' he corrected.

She nodded slowly.

'You must have had servants?'

'God, no.' She laughed, having no idea how beautiful she looked as the creamy midday sun bounced across her blonde hair, causing it to shimmer. 'My father hated the idea of having people in our home. He's very private.'

At the reference to Lionel Howard something between them shifted, a darkness descending on the table.

Gabe spoke first with a heavy sigh. 'Tell me how it started.'

Abby lifted her shoulders. 'How what started?'

'You, coming to meet me. What did your father say to you?'

Abby's tummy twisted. She couldn't meet his eyes. 'Is that why you wanted to have lunch with me?'

Gabe's frown was infinitesimal, but she caught the tail end of it.

'It's natural you'd be curious,' she rushed to add.

'I wasn't. But seeing as you've mentioned him…'

She nodded. Hadn't she decided that she needed to be honest with him, to help him understand why she'd done what she had? Of course he felt the same need to know.

'I told you—' she spoke slowly, every word considered '—my father was destroyed when your company launched.' Her grimace was an acknowledgement of the fact that this was an awkward conversation to have. 'I'd heard about you for years, you know.'

She felt Gabe stiffen without looking at him.

'He came to blame you and…your foster brother…for every single business problem he had.' She closed her eyes, finding it insufficient simply to look away from Gabe now and needing instead to block him out completely. Her slender throat shifted as she swallowed.

'You are not saying anything I had not deduced for myself,' he said. The words were offered with his usual degree of detachment but Abby felt them—she felt them right in the centre of her heart. 'You are fortunate your father targeted me rather than Noah.'

'Why?'

Gabe thought of his best friend and his frown deepened. 'Because Noah is…'

She waited, her interest obvious.

'Noah and I are very similar. But he has no interest in pretending to be civil. He would have chewed you up and spat you back out again if you'd tried your trick on him.'

'It wasn't a trick.'

He ignored her. 'Noah would have seen through you too. He's always been a better judge of character than me.'

She paled.

'He would hate you, I think, for what you planned to do.'

Abby gripped the fork tightly, her brain hurting. 'I'm sorry to hear that. He's your best friend, right?'

'He's my…yes.'

'Have you told him about us? About Raf?'

Gabe's eyes held Abby's. 'No.'

'Why not?'

'He's…' Gabe looked towards the window for a moment, his expression tight. 'He's got his own stuff going on.' It was vague enough to create more questions than it answered, but Abby didn't push him. Gabe had clammed up and she knew him well enough to know that he would only speak when he was ready to share.

'My dad didn't *target* you,' she said softly, bringing them back to the topic.

Gabe spun back to face her, lancing her with his eyes.

'He wanted information. He never meant to hurt you.'

'He wanted to destroy my business. You don't think that would have hurt me?'

'He didn't think about it like that,' Abby insisted. 'You were irrelevant. All he cares about is his own success. For years he was at the top of his game, and then you came along…'

'I am hardly irrelevant, given that he sent you to spy on me.'

She brushed past his interruption impatiently. 'But do you understand what I'm saying?'

'I understand the excuses you're offering.' His eyes glittered with an emotion she didn't understand and then, as though the words were being dragged from him, 'I believe you were motivated by love for your father rather than hatred for me.'

'Hatred?' That jolted her eyes to his and she reached across the table, curving her palm over his. 'It was *never* about hatred for you. Even before I met you I was *fascinated* by you, Gabe. Your... dynamism and success, your work ethic, your lifestyle.' She blushed. 'You were my polar opposite in every way. It didn't take much convincing when my dad suggested I meet you...'

He swallowed, his throat bunching beneath her gaze. 'And yet you still came with the intention of finding whatever information you could and taking it back to your father?'

She bit down on her lip, nodding slowly.

At his look of disapproval, she rushed to add, 'But only at first. Gabe, fifteen minutes into knowing you and there was no way I was going to go through with it.'

She withdrew her hand, the intimacy feeling discordant suddenly. 'I slept with you because I wanted to,' she said with quiet insistence.

'You wanted me? You wanted Calypso.'

'No!' She shook her head to emphatically refute him. 'Gabe, you have to believe me. Us sleeping together, that was... Didn't you feel it?'

'Feel what, *tempesta?*' he challenged stonily, every cell in his body closed to her, the definition of immovable.

Still, having come this far, Abby urged herself to be honest. 'A connection,' she said, her eyes landing on his. 'I felt something for you the instant you spoke to me, the second we first touched, when you made me laugh… I *wanted* you to be my first lover,' she promised. 'Because of who you were to *me*, not to Dad, nor to the world.'

He was quiet, appraising her words from every angle.

'You told me you simply wanted to rid yourself of your tiresome virginity,' he pointed out.

Inwardly she winced, wishing she could take back that excuse. She'd said it to save some pride, but now she wanted to dispel that idea. 'You don't think I'd been smiled at by handsome men before?' she asked. 'You don't think I'd had ample opportunities to "rid myself" of my virginity in the past?'

He stared at her long and hard, his cheeks darkening with a flush of emotion. 'I don't know.' He shrugged. 'It made little sense to me on that night; it still doesn't.'

'I had no interest in sex,' she said simply. 'I was too busy with ballet—my schedule was pretty intensive—and then, by the time I gave it up, when it came to intimacy I felt like a fish out of water. All my friends had been in several relationships, and the guys I met were obviously way more experienced. I was…embarrassed.'

'You weren't with me.'

'Because I felt like I knew you,' she said with urgency. Had he truly not felt that same sense of familiarity?

'Abigail—' he sighed heavily, dragging his fingertips through his hair '—I think you need to be careful here.'

'Careful how?' she prompted.

'You speak like a classic romantic,' he said, his smile bordering on mocking. 'A connection. As though I was some fated Prince Charming riding into town to win your heart.' He laughed, a harsh sound, but that same heart ratcheted up a gear, his description unknowingly hitting on how she *had* felt at the time. 'We are going to get married, *for our son.* The last thing I want is for you to get hurt—even if a small part of me thinks you are simply reaping what you sowed a year ago.'

Pain scored Abby deep in her heart and her veins turned to ice as crisply cold as the snow outside. 'I've tried to explain—'

'Damn it! Abigail, listen to me.' He softened his tone with obvious effort. 'You will never be able to explain what you did. What you intended to do. I appreciate that you didn't follow through with what your father wanted, but you came to me with one purpose—betrayal. Nothing that happened beyond that matters. Had you not fallen pregnant, if we didn't share a son, we wouldn't be sitting across a table having this conversation. Or any conversation. You understand that, don't you?'

She sat frozen to the spot, her heart thumping inside her the only sign of life. His words were shredding her into tiny pieces and uncertainty lurched all around her. 'How can you say that?' she asked quietly, digging her fingernails into her palms. 'After what we shared the other day?'

His smile was almost sympathetic. 'For your own good, try to remember that sex and love are two very distinct sides of a coin.'

His words ran around her head like an angry tornado. She didn't believe it was *love*, necessarily, but it was more than just great sex. When they were together she felt as if she could trust him with her life; she felt as if everything made sense. Didn't he feel that too? Or did he always feel that?

'I guess I wouldn't know,' she said after a moment, hoping she didn't sound as confused as she felt. 'You, on the other hand, have plenty of experience.'

'Yes.' The word was a crisp agreement. He reached over and topped up Abby's wine; she hadn't even realised she'd been sipping it as they spoke. 'Was he angry when you went home empty-handed?'

It took Abby a moment to realise that Gabe had

returned to their original topic of conversation. 'Yes.' She didn't feel like talking about her father though. 'You were fostered in Australia?' she asked, the question catching Gabe off-guard. His face shifted into a mask of displeasure but he covered it quickly enough.

'Yes.'

'But you were born here? In Italy?'

'Yes.'

Abby frowned. 'So how did you end up in Australia? I would have thought you would stay in your own country when you lost your mother...'

'She had recently emigrated to Australia,' he said matter-of-factly. 'It's where she was from, and she still had family there. A cousin, at least. It made sense to go home.'

'How did she die?' The question sounded insensitive even to Abby's ears. She blamed the wine and the fact she was still reeling from the ease with which he'd limited their relationship simply to sex...

'A drug overdose,' Gabe said, the words cold.

'I'm sorry.' She reached over, cupping her hand over his. 'That must have been awful.'

'Awful?' He looked at her hand as though it were a foreign object, something unexpected and strange on the table. 'Awful is one way to describe it.'

'Were you close to her?'

Gabe's eyes lanced Abby. 'Aren't all children close to their mothers?'

Abby nodded. 'I guess.' She was quiet as she contemplated her next question.

'You can ask,' he prompted, understanding that she was holding back.

'Had she taken drugs for long?'

'No.' He reached for his wine and took a sip. The silence around them was another presence at the table, heavy and sad, all-encompassing.

It was broken by the arrival of a domestic, wheeling in a trolley laden with food. Plate after plate was placed on the table and silence didn't give way. Abby watched Gabe from beneath shuttered lashes, studying him, trying to imagine him as a heartbroken eight-year-old.

When the servant left and the food was offering delicious, tantalising aromas, Abby spoke again. 'Did you know she had a substance abuse problem?'

Gabe was stiff. 'I was only a child,' he said, his broad shoulders lifting with self-recrimination. 'I suppose I knew something was wrong, but I had no way of knowing exactly what. It started about a year before we moved to Australia.' His expression was taut, his whole body wound like a spring. 'It got worse once we arrived.'

Abby shifted in her chair and, beneath the table, her toe inadvertently rubbed against his calf. His eyes seared hers with the heat that was always simmering just below the surface for them.

But Abby didn't want to be distracted by what they felt physically. She sensed that she was on the brink of understanding something important. Something important about Gabe that she *needed* to know.

'Why?'

She felt the depth of emotion in him and wanted to reach inside him and hold it, to reassure him and comfort him. But she couldn't without knowing what motivated it.

'You want me to explain addiction?' he asked, but the question didn't come across as flippant as Abby knew he'd hoped. It was desperate. Angry. She could see the eight-year-old he'd been now, feel his sense of rejection.

'Your mother's addiction,' she said quietly. 'Do you know why she took drugs?'

He sat straighter in his chair, as though remembering that he was Gabe Arantini, one half of the multi-billion-dollar Bright Spark Inc, a man renowned the world over as a ruthless CEO. 'I know why she was miserable.'

'Why?'

His eyes pierced hers then and she shivered because there was such cold anger in his gaze that it scored her deep inside. 'Because she made the phenomenally stupid mistake of falling in love with my father.'

She felt his words resonate strongly: a warning to herself.

'They weren't happy together?' Abby pushed. The feeling that she was on the brink of something very important held her still.

'They weren't together at all, period.'

Abby frowned, remembering threads of past conversations. 'You told me that you destroyed your father...'

'Yes.' He nodded once, a cold jerk of his head.

'He hurt her?'

'He ruined her life,' Gabe grunted.

'How? Why?'

'Because I hardly fitted into his plans, *tempesta.*'

'He didn't want to be a father?'

'He was already a father,' Gabe corrected. 'A grandfather too.'

Abby frowned. 'I don't understand.'

Gabe expelled an angry sigh, and now his eyes held resentment. 'My mother was a cleaner. Here. In this castle.' He waved a hand around the room. 'My father was a lecherous jerk who liked to get his hands on the maids when his wife wasn't looking—which was pretty often.'

Abby frowned, but she didn't say anything. She

didn't want to interrupt him. Not now that he'd started to open up.

'She *loved* him. When she found out she was pregnant, she was overjoyed,' Gabe spat, his derision for that emotion obvious.

'He wasn't overjoyed, though,' she surmised.

'No.' Gabe sipped his wine then turned his head, his eyes running over the view through the window. The snow was still falling—a thicker layer had settled on the railing now. 'He paid her to have an abortion. And fired her.'

Abby gasped. She couldn't help it. 'You're not serious?'

He didn't answer. Her question had been largely rhetorical.

'She took the money and tried to make a life for herself in a nearby village.' His eyes shifted to Abby's for a moment. 'It was tough. Being a single mother to an infant is not easy, as you are well aware.'

Something was prickling at the edges of Abby's brain, something she didn't want to think about until later. But it offered darkness and doubt and complications she hadn't been aware of when she'd agreed to this.

'What did she do?'

'She blackmailed him,' Gabe said softly. 'He paid a small amount to keep her quiet and refused to see us. I don't think she even wanted the money,' he said. 'She wanted him to be in our lives. She really did love him. He was forty-five years older than her and he'd had a string of affairs. He was an out-and-out bastard to her, by all accounts. Apparently love makes people act like fools.'

'Eventually, as he grew older, I suppose he became worried about what would happen when he died. Would my mother seek a share of his inheritance?'

'She'd have been entitled!' Abby snapped, ignoring the parallels between her own situation and that of Gabe's mother.

'Yes.' His gaze narrowed thoughtfully on Abby. 'But she wouldn't have tried. As I said, she loved him.'

'So what happened?'

'He convinced her to go back to her home. He bought her ticket, told her he would come and see us, that if we were over there it would be easier for him to visit and be in our lives. He offered her a lot of money to leave Italy.'

Gabe's face was taut with anger. 'He lied to her. He wanted her gone. He knew he would never visit, but he also knew that once she was in Australia it would be harder for her to come here.'

'But he gave her money...'

'He *promised* to give her money. It never eventuated. Once she landed he broke it off.'

'Oh, God.'

'So I can only presume it caused her to do whatever she could to blot out the pain.'

'Gabe…' Abby's heart was swelling with sympathy and sorrow for both his mother and him—then and now. 'That's awful.'

Gabe's nod was a sharp dismissal. 'He was a bastard, as I said.'

'But he must have had a change of heart,' Abby said thoughtfully. 'To leave you the castle…'

'Leave it to me?' Gabe let out a harsh laugh. 'He was in his nineties when I bought it from him. His finances had been draining for years. The castle was all he had left.'

Something like pure hatred flashed in his face. 'I took it from him for her, you know. I wanted my father to die knowing that I was living here.'

'Oh, Gabe…' She squeezed her eyes shut. 'I'm so sorry.'

'Why? I did what I needed. I made him pay. I avenged her life and death, her abuse at my father's hands. I only wish his wife had lived to learn about me.'

A shiver ran down Abby's spine; Gabe's hatred and animosity were formidable. She couldn't imagine being on the receiving end of that degree of rage. It made his anger with her, her intention to deceive him, pale in comparison.

'Did he know she'd died? That you were left alone out there?'

'Yes.'

Abby's eyes swept shut. The rejection was awful and astounding.

'So you see why it is very important to me that Raf grows up knowing his parents love and want him; why I want him to see that I live to protect him, to protect you both. I never wish him to have a reason to doubt that.' His frown deepened. 'You must also understand that if I had known about him sooner I would have done everything I could to spare you the pain and financial burden you carried. I would have made sure you were comfortable and cared for, that you had all you needed. I would never allow a woman to experience what my mother did.'

Abby nodded, but it was impossible to take any comfort from his words. He wanted to do right by her but not because of who she was, nor because of the connection she was convinced they shared. No, this was all because of what had happened to his mother. The concern she'd allowed herself to see, to hope might be a sign of burgeoning feelings specifically for her, was simply a commitment to a duty he knew his father had neglected.

Tears sparkled on her lashes and she blinked them away hurriedly, but not fast enough to escape the notice of Gabe.

'It was a long time ago,' he said softly, misunderstanding the reason for her emotional response. 'Getting upset won't change what happened then.'

She nodded, dashing at her cheeks with fingertips that weren't quite steady.

'You met Noah through foster care?'

'Yes. I'd been in the system a long time by then,' he said, the conversation obviously one he wasn't overly thrilled to be having. 'The day he arrived at the same house was a turning point for me. And for him.' He shifted in his seat. 'Eat something, Abigail. You are too slim.'

She frowned. Was she? She had always been petite—her ballerina build partly genetics as well as from diet and exercise. But since having Raf she'd been stretched emotionally and financially. 'I don't always get time to eat,' she admitted.

'You've been busy. Raising a child on your own must have been difficult.'

Gabe reached for some serving spoons and began to heap various portions onto her plate. She watched with a frown. 'You could say that.'

'And the pregnancy?'

She blinked. 'Hard. I was sick often.'

He shook his head. 'I should have been there.'

'You couldn't have done anything to stop me from being ill,' she pointed out, her heart thumping hard in her chest.

'I tried to tell you,' she said, though they'd discussed it before. 'About Raf. I *wanted* you to be involved.'

His eyes locked onto hers and something strong and fierce surged between them, an electrical current that flooded her body with sensations. 'I know that.' He compressed his lips into a grim line. 'And it's just as well. I can't think how I might have reacted if you'd chosen to conceal my child from me. I think that is something I would *never* have been able to overlook.'

She swallowed. 'You'd probably feel a little like I did when I was dragged out of your office in Rome,' she said tartly.

He winced. 'A grave error on my part.' His eyes held hers. 'I am sorry, *tempesta*. I should have listened to you.'

How could she fail to be moved by his apology? She lowered her lashes to the meal and speared a piece of vegetable, but inside she was warming up from the centre.

But not for long.

'I could have killed your father, you know,' he said, so conversationally that Abby almost laughed. Except it wasn't funny—not even remotely.

'He was the man who should have been there for you, who should have loved you, and he was no better than my own father. He threw you out into the cold—and threw Raf out too. How you can *not* hate him is beyond me.'

She shook her head sadly. 'Because he's my father,' she said simply. 'And I see him for what he is. Flawed, yes. Broken, undoubtedly. But there is goodness in him too, and kindness. He's just been too battered by life's ill winds to remember that.'

Gabe let out a noise of frustration. 'You make excuses for him because you are not brave enough to face the truth and accept that he is a disappointment. You are too frightened to live in a world in which you reject your father.'

'I think it takes more courage to fight for who you love,' she said with quiet strength. 'To hold onto the truth of what you believe, deep in your heart, even when all evidence is to the contrary. I *know* my dad. I know how he feels. I understand why he acts as he does. And I forgive him that.'

He swore. 'Do me a favour, Abigail? Never say such things about me. Never make excuses for me as though I need them. I know I am cold and ruthless and cynical—my father's son in many ways—and that I am—and always will be—a loner in this life. I am happy with that. I don't need you digging deeper and pretending there is more to me.'

'A loner?' she murmured, the smile on her lips heavy. 'Hardly. You're a father, and soon to be a husband.'

'Yes,' he said with a curt nod. 'But our marriage is not about love; it is about common sense and practicality. Isn't that proof of my coldness?'

CHAPTER ELEVEN

ABBY BARELY TASTED the scampi, though she was sure they were delicious. Everything looked to have been prepared with care and using only the finest ingredients, but her mind was reeling.

It shouldn't have surprised her. She knew that what Gabe said was true. And yet her own visceral sense of despondency forced her to look deeper and acknowledge what she'd probably known all along.

Why had she been willing—no, desperate!—to go to bed with him? Because the connection she'd felt was that mythical, much talked about love at first sight. She'd looked at Gabe and known that they were meant to be together. That there was more to their meeting than a random happenstance and her father's financially motivated manipulations.

It was him and her.

Fate had conspired to give them a baby, linking them for ever. Surely there had been something predestined and magical at work there, for now that she knew the story of his parentage she didn't doubt that Gabe would *always* take great care not to conceive a child.

'I'm sorry you have been worried about money,'

he said, apparently having no idea that Abby was still brooding over his revelations.

'Yeah, well, working in a kitchen doesn't pay very well.'

'I don't mean in New York,' he said. 'I'm talking about here in Italy.' His frown was grim, self-condemnatory. 'I overlooked this detail, and I truly regret that.' He reached into the bag beside him and pulled out a black wallet, slender and long.

'I've had cards drawn in your name.' He passed the wallet to Abby and she opened it reflexively. 'You'll have no spending limit, of course. Buy whatever you need.'

The words were said without any expectation of a response but Abby sharply rejected the sentiment.

'There's cash too.' He nodded, indicating a huge wad of hundred euro bills. 'And I'll have one of my assistants take on your workload. Anything you need—money, holidays booked, cars, if you wish to go back to America and see…your father, or anyone, she will arrange.'

A shiver ran down Abby's spine. The delineation was clear—she was his wife in name only. Oh, and in his bed. But when it came to troubling himself with her concerns, he was washing his hands of it.

Abby folded the wallet and placed it in the centre of the table. 'I don't need any of that.'

He leaned forward. 'You have already proved to me that you are not mercenary, but think this through, Abigail. Do you want to come and ask me for money any time you want to book a trip? To go on holiday?'

She swept her eyes shut. She had thought, of course, stupidly, that they would do such trips together. But of course Gabe was setting out a life that was far more private. Separate.

A loner in this life.

Her heart twisted. Just like that, the difficulty of her position became glaringly obvious. She had fought it, she had resisted, but such efforts had proved impossible. She was in love with him and he felt *nothing* for her, beyond responsibility. He was trying to right the wrongs of the past, to prove to himself that he was different to his father, Lorenzo.

Her future yawned before her, long and cold, save for the love of their son. Raf alone could make this bearable for her.

'I want you to make a life here with me,' he said gently, so that her heart ached. 'A real life. You aren't to feel like a guest. This is your house, your money. Our son binds us, *tempesta.*'

'*Tempesta,*' she said distractedly. 'You call me that often. What does it mean?'

'Storm.' His lips twisted sardonically. 'I thought it the first night we met—that you had the power to move through me like a hurricane. I feel that still.'

She wouldn't let those words come to mean anything. They were insufficient, meaningless.

'Have you told your father we are to marry?'

Abigail shook her head. 'I didn't have time before I left and…' The words trailed off into nothingness.

'You don't want him to know,' Gabe concluded.

'He'd hate this,' she said simply. 'I'd worry that it would be the last straw for him. You know? Since losing Mom, he's just been so…caught up in the company and a huge part of that is…'

'Hating me,' Gabe supplied with a drawl.

'Yes.' No sense denying that. 'When he found out I was pregnant with Raf, that you were the father, it was like I'd shot him.'

Gabe's eyes narrowed.

'Knowing that I've moved in with you… I don't want to do that to him.'

Sheer cold anger met her gaze when she looked at him. He was furious—but why? 'Do you expect our marriage will be kept out of the public eye? I am a well-known figure, and you are too. At some point the media will discover our union. Isn't it better for your father to hear it first from us?'

'No.' She shook her head quickly. 'Absolutely not. It's best of all if he *never* knows.'

'But I've just pointed out how unlikely that is.'

'Unlikely isn't definite,' she said urgently. 'There's still a chance.'

* * *

The noise was shrill, panicked. He sat bolt upright, rubbing a hand across his face, trying to work out what the hell was going on. He turned around and saw her. Abby, crying out in her sleep. He stared at her and an adrenal response fired in his belly. He reached for her, shaking her shoulder gently. 'Wake up, Abby.'

She pulled a face in her sleep but didn't open her eyes.

'You're dreaming.'

She mumbled something, words he didn't hear, so he did the only thing he could. He kissed her, swallowing the panic, tasting it, and returning it as passion. She responded instantly, wrapping her arms around his neck and, when he lifted his head a little, her eyes were open. Groggy and thick with passionate entreaty.

His own body stirred in response, but his curiosity over what had upset her was greater. 'You were having a nightmare.'

'Was I?' Her eyes flicked away from his, a small frown playing about her lips. He dropped a finger to them, touching her gently. 'That happens sometimes.'

That adrenaline response was back. 'Does it?'

'Not for a long time.' She cleared her throat. 'It started when my mom died.'

Gabe dropped onto the pillow beside her, propping himself on one elbow so he could see her face. 'Are the nightmares about your mother?'

'Yes and no.' She slid her gaze to him warily. 'She's always in them, but out of reach. Like watching me from behind a window or talking to me but when I look for her I can't find her. Does that make sense?'

He shrugged. 'Dreams rarely do.'

'I haven't had one in a long time.' She swallowed. 'But I've been thinking about her a lot lately. She would have loved Raf, you know.'

He smiled, but inside he felt as if she'd hit him hard. No, not her, it was life. He didn't want his wife to be miserable; he didn't want her to be mourning a mother she'd so obviously loved. He couldn't fix that, though. Death was life's most final act—what could be done to remedy it?

'Do you…?' Abby swallowed. 'You must miss your mother.'

Gabe shrugged a single shoulder. 'I miss the role she might have played in my life.'

'It must have been so hard for you.' Abby lifted a hand and traced an invisible circle on his shoulder, almost against her will. 'To have seen your mother so miserable, to have known your father to be the cause…'

'She was the cause,' he said softly. 'She should have seen what he was doing to her and fled. She should have taken whatever money he'd given her and left him, and started a new life.'

'Starting a new life isn't easy. And it sounds like your father led her on, like he led her to believe he might love her too.'

'Yes.' Gabe's eyes sparkled with renewed determination. He was nothing like his own father—he had never led Abby on. In this way, they were vitally different.

'Go to sleep, *tempesta*. And try to make your dreams sweet.'

And though she had a habit of creeping to her own bed in the middle of the night, he slid his arm beneath her, rolling her onto his chest so he could feel her breathing and hold her tight. He couldn't bring her mother back to life but, with any luck, he could forestall the nightmares.

That, at least, was within his power.

Gabe stared out of his study window without seeing the vista. He was used to it and, despite the fact he had, once upon a time, thought this to be the most beautiful place on earth, he had grown accustomed to its charms now. Did that diminish it, somehow?

He had also grown accustomed to having Abby in his bed. He was used to all of her belonging to him, utterly and completely, though it had only been days since his return from Rome.

She didn't hide how much she wanted him, and he was glad for that.

He had worried she would mistake their chemistry and marriage for love, but she seemed to understand that theirs was a transaction and only certain parts of him were on the table.

But at night, oh, how he craved her.

He doubted that need would ever fade, his appreciation for her curves and undulations unlikely to diminish with exposure.

In fact, the opposite was true. The more that he was with her, the more he wanted her. He woke up aching to pull her close, but with the sun's rise came the reality of their situation and everything shifted between them. She pulled away from him, presenting him with a cool smile and a terse nod, showering in her own en suite bathroom, away from him, away from his touch and kiss and eyes that were hungry for more glimpses of her beautiful body.

She spent much of her time with Raf, even just reading in his room. He knew because Monique had become worried for Abby.

'She seems distracted and tired. She doesn't need to exhaust herself with the baby—she must have more important things to do! Weddings don't plan themselves.'

But Abby had no interest in planning a wedding. She had told him outright that she was happy to organise things, but that her preference was for as small a ceremony as possible, just the two of them and Raf, with a couple of domestics as witnesses. No guests, no dinner. When he'd suggested a honeymoon she'd blanched and pointed out in a brittle voice that they were already living as a married couple. Besides, she'd added with a poor attempt at a smile, where in the world could they go more idyllic than the castle?

He'd analysed the feeling low in his abdomen for days, wondering at its root cause, but now he had to admit it. He was ill at ease.

He'd brought Abigail to Italy with the belief that it would be best for her, and him, as well as Raf, and she seemed to be fading away before his eyes. She'd thrown herself into the Christmas spirit, adding little touches throughout the house, like green garlands along the staircase, the Christmas tree she'd decorated with the lone bauble, food that she baked that had an unmistakably Christmas aroma. That had been the only sign she was settling into life in Italy. That she was making her peace with being here, with him.

What had she said the day they'd argued about Hughie? *He's nice to me…*

Something uncomfortable shifted inside Gabe. Nice? He wasn't sure he knew how to be *nice*. He wasn't sure he knew how to be anything Abby needed.

A knock at his door roused him from his thoughts. He turned around, expecting to see one of his staff. Only it was Abby and, as always, his body responded instantly to her appearance. His blood began to rush through him, tightening him, making him throb and ache for her anew, and his eyes ran over her hungrily, needily, desperately.

She blushed beneath his inspection.

'Am I interrupting?'

'Not at all.' He indicated the seat opposite him, but she shook her head.

'This won't take long.'

'What is it?' He came around to the opposite side of the desk and propped his hips against it. He saw the way her eyes darted to his haunches and the way his trousers had strained across the muscles there, and something like relief filled him.

She wanted him.

And she always would. In bed, she wasn't cold—ever. She begged for him and dragged her nails down his back and nipped at his flesh; in bed she was a fever in his blood, because that same fever raged in her blood.

It wasn't *nice*. It was so much better.

'I know Raf is only little, but this will be his first Christmas and I want it to be special. He won't remember it, I know,' she rushed on, countering her sentimentality before he could. That she knew him so well worried him.

'But he'll have photos—we can have photos, I mean, get them framed and put them in his room. You want him to have a family—' now she forced her eyes to his and he felt their defiance '—and I do too. I want him to know we've been a family since he was born.'

He nodded thoughtfully.

He'd been doing that a lot lately.

Thinking.

Thinking about Abby and the things she'd said. She was like a fever in his blood and he resented her for that, even while knowing it was hardly her fault. He simply had to try harder to regain control of the situation.

'Anyway—' she was awkward '—I wondered if I could somehow get to Fiamatina today, or tomorrow, to buy him a little gift.' Colour filled her cheeks, two dots of pink on either side of her lips. 'I don't mean anything grand, just a book or a little toy. He doesn't need much, obviously. It's more about giving him something we can keep for him.'

Gabe was struck by this—more so by the fact it hadn't even occurred to him, despite the way she'd turned his house into Santa's Grotto, that Christmas might mean something to Abby. That, unlike his terrible memories of this time of year, she might actually *want* to mark the day in a manner that was different to any other.

'Fiamatina.' He jerked his head. 'I'll take you.'
And if he had any luck he'd find the perfect present for her. She should have something to open,
seeing as the day meant so much to her.

'Oh!' Her surprise was obvious, so too her dismissal. 'You don't have to take me. You're busy.
I can drive.'

He laughed, a grim rejection of that idea. 'Do
you have any experience of driving on snow or
ice, Abigail?'

Her eyes met his, annoyance brimming in their
depths. At least that was better than coldness. 'No,
but I'll be careful.'

'You must be mad if you think I would let you
risk your life like that.'

'*You* must be mad if you think I'd ever do anything dangerous, that I wasn't capable of. I'll be
fine.'

'I intend to make sure of it.' He put a hand at the
crook of her elbow. 'Are you ready?'

'Have I told you how bossy you are?'

'I think so.'

She glared at him. 'You're busy and I have to
learn to drive here at some point—'

'Perhaps. But not today.'

She fired him a fulminating glare and he ignored the jolt of pleasure in his gut. The relief of
seeing her emotional response. He'd take her anger
over ice-coldness any day of the week.

He liked her being emotional; he liked knowing he'd caused that. He was addicted to it.

With a throaty sound of need, he curved his hand from her elbow to her back, pulling her to him, and when her eyes flew wide in surprise and her lips parted on a gasp he kissed her, pushing her back against the door to his office, his body holding hers.

She was his in an instant, her hands lifting to link behind his head, her hips moving, swaying in time to their kiss and the sensual fog that always pursued them.

She was wearing a dress, thank God, as opposed to her usual jeans, and he lifted it desperately, finding the sweet curve of her bottom, cupping it in his hands and lifting her so that her legs wrapped around his waist and his arousal pressed hard to her, hungry for her as always.

He spoke in Italian, words he couldn't have recalled later, words that came from deep within him, whispering them in her ear as his fingers pushed her underwear aside and found the heart of her warmth, sliding inside her until she bucked against him.

'Please,' she groaned, breaking the kiss to look into his eyes. 'I need you, Gabe. I need this. Please.'

He understood and it was instinct alone that pushed him, his hands freeing his arousal from his trousers, just enough to take her, to hold her to him, to bind them together.

She was panting against him, kissing him frantically, her hands running over his shoulders and arms, her body trembling until finally they both exploded in unison, one singular, perfect release for the *tempesta* that had been raging between them—and probably always would.

'Oh, my God,' Abby murmured as sanity began to seep back into her passion-addled brain. 'What just happened?'

Gabe straightened, his smile one of such indulgence that her heart tripped heavily inside her. 'Well, we've done it before. Quite often. I presumed you understood…'

'We didn't use protection.' She dipped her head so that her forehead was pressed to his shoulder. 'That was so stupid.'

'Stupid? I can think of other words to describe it.'

'You don't understand,' she groaned. 'I'm not on any form of contraception.'

Comprehension dawned, but apparently produced a very different reaction for Gabe. 'So?' he asked, a brow lifted. 'Then we have another baby.'

'Another baby?' Her words were a sharp rejection of the idea. She pushed away from him, placing her feet on the ground and straightening her dress with fingers that shook. Panic seared her belly.

'Yes, another baby. Two more. Three more. We already have Raf. We're getting married. Why not more children?'

'How can you be so cavalier about this?'

'Calm down, *tempesta*. You're acting as though this is the worst thing in the world. You don't even know if there will be any…complications…'

'It *would* be the worst thing in the world!' Abby shouted, the stress and the confusion of the last few weeks beginning to mount inside her, so that she was pale, her eyes flashing with emotion.

In contrast, Gabe was completely frozen, his expression like granite. 'Why, may I ask, is that?'

She bit down on her lip and looked over his shoulder. How could she explain how she felt? How could she put into words the misgivings she had? About this wedding, their marriage, the ability to raise Raf in a way that wouldn't completely mess him up? Another baby would be heaven on earth if they were a real couple. 'It's irresponsible to bring another baby into this environment,' she said crisply. 'Raf happened, and we're getting married to give him a family. But there's no sense compounding that with any more children. Raf is enough.'

CHAPTER TWELVE

GABE USED VOICE-COMMAND to call his best friend.

'Noah?' His voice was gruff when the call connected.

'Gabe. What's up?'

Gabe swallowed, staring at his desk. An excellent question.

'I just wanted to see how you are,' he lied anxiously. Noah had enough going on in his life—he didn't need Gabe adding to it.

'Fine. I'm cured, remember?'

Gabe frowned. The therapy he'd made Noah enter might have been paying dividends. But wasn't it too soon? Gabe silenced the doubts. He wanted to believe his foster brother was improving. He wanted to feel some degree of relief.

'I'm glad.' Gabe sighed heavily. 'I'm…' He clamped his lips together. What did he want to say? *I'm getting married.* No. Too problematic. Noah would want to know what the hell had happened. Gabe had sworn until he was blue in the face that he would *never* marry. He'd promised himself repeatedly that emotional commitments were for fools; he'd sworn to be smart.

And he *was* being smart. This marriage wasn't about emotion.

'Do you ever wonder what the Sloanes are doing?'

'Those bastards? No. I never think of them.' The anger in Noah's voice made a liar of him. Their foster family had influenced both their lives, no matter how they wished that weren't the case.

Gabe pushed back in the leather chair, his eyes closed.

'Why? Do you?'

Gabe frowned. 'I was with them a lot longer. They're almost the only family I remember.' The words were defensive and immediately a response came to him. He saw, in his mind's eye, the mother of his son. The woman he would marry. And his gut twisted. He'd been given a family at birth—a father who didn't want him, a mother who resented him.

He'd been taken in by a family—they hadn't wanted him either.

And now? A sense of unease tripped through him. Being unwanted was the running theme of his life—and now he was marrying a woman who wanted more than he could give her. He was marrying a woman who deserved more.

'They were bastards,' Noah grunted. 'I hope they got what was coming to them.'

Gabe's lips compressed. 'I don't.'

'You always were a soft touch.'

At that, Gabe laughed. If only Noah knew what

he was about to do. Abby had been cast out of her life, left pregnant and impoverished, abandoned by her father, orphaned by her mother, and he'd strong-armed her at every point. He'd swept aside her objections. He'd insisted on this—and he'd been right. Marriage was the only option. But suddenly the idea of joining himself legally to Abby seemed absurd. She didn't want him, not as he was, and he didn't want her. Did he?

They'd slept together a long time ago, and that had been a mistake. She had used him, she had lied to him, she had gone to him specifically to further her father's business interests. He had no business wanting her—other than physically.

This marriage wasn't about anything other than practicality, and giving their son what he deserved, just like Abigail had said. Raf wouldn't grow up wondering about his father, resenting his father, hating his father. He wouldn't feel for Gabe as Gabe had for Lorenzo. No, Raf would feel loved. He would feel cherished and he would feel wanted.

And he just had to hope he wouldn't ruin Abby's life in the process. No matter what she'd done, no matter how he told himself he'd never forgive her, he knew the truth. He didn't want to hurt her; he didn't want to ruin her life.

He wasn't his father, he reminded himself, even when his doubts made his conviction waver. They would marry and Gabe would make sure she had a good life. A great life.

He wouldn't be the kind of husband she wanted nor deserved, but eventually she'd get over that. Wouldn't she?

Christmas morning at the castle was spectacular in all ways but one. Snow had begun to fall overnight and Hughie, who'd gone home to see his family, wasn't around to clear it, which meant the place seemed even more magical than ever, as though it had risen from the edge of the mountains. A little family of squirrels ran across the field and Abby watched them, an enchanted smile on her face as they scampered up a tree. As for their Christmas tree, the lights glistened in the early morning sunshine as the smell of coffee filled the hall.

Raf slept in a bassinet at Abby's feet as she lost herself to the pages of *Persuasion*—her favourite of all the Austens. There was something about Captain Wentworth's enduring love for Anne Elliot that had always spoken to her.

No doubt, Gabe would accuse her of over-sentimentality, but she had always adored the idea of such permanence. The idea that years spent apart, with one at war and the other marooned by a cold, unemotional family, couldn't destroy true love.

Abby's eyes lifted to where Gabe sat, reading a newspaper on his tablet, apparently absorbed. Yes, it was all spectacular, save for the tension that was zapping between them.

Her heart raced and her skin goosed all over. She drew in a deep breath and told herself she'd be fine, that she could do this. Reminding herself that they were celebrating for Raf.

She was the one who'd put this in motion—now wasn't the time to start having regrets.

Their marriage would work just fine. The longer they were together, the better she'd get at pretending not to feel anything for Gabe.

He'd put presents beneath the tree, though, and her heart skipped a beat. Were they for Raf? Surely they must be. Not for her...

Her eyes strayed to the tree, a frown on her face. Nothing was labelled. 'Yes, *tempesta*. It's for you.'

'Oh!' She spun to face him, her cheeks flushed. 'I didn't get you anything.'

'It's a gift for both of us.'

She frowned. 'Shall I open it now?'

Something glowed in his eyes. 'Raf is awake. Why don't we get that photo you wanted before he drifts off again?'

Abby nodded. 'All the staff are upstairs. Shall I...'

'I can take it.' He pulled his cell phone from his pocket and propped it on a ledge near the door, then stepped back towards Abby. She held Raf in her arms, smiling down at him, leaving Gabe to take the space beside her. Using his watch, he set the timer going. A light on the phone flashed faster and faster.

'Ready?' Gabe asked after a moment.

She nodded and forced a smile to her face, breathing in her husband, her baby, their first Christmas together. The phone clicked, just like an old-fashioned camera, taking the photo, so they'd always have a photograph with which to remember this moment. Abby didn't break the pose though. Just for that small fraction of time, she let herself pretend that this was all real. Normal.

That Gabe was marrying her because he wanted to, that Raf had been conceived in love. Emotion hitched, heavy, in her throat. It was Christmas; couldn't she wish?

'Gabe…' She looked up at him, not entirely sure what she wanted to say. Their eyes locked and she felt the force of her emotions throbbing around them, so strong and urgent that she wasn't sure she could ignore them. She knew she didn't want to.

'Open your present,' he suggested, taking Raf from her arms. He held their baby so naturally, as though he'd been doing it all his life, and Abby could only watch, those same emotions intensifying at the proof of Raf's parentage.

'He's so like you.'

'He's my son.'

She nodded, spinning away from him. The cloying feelings were heavy inside her, swirling like the hurricane he often called her. Now that she knew how she felt about him, it was impossible not to be conscious of it whenever they were together. She walked towards the gift—it was large in size. A box of something?

'Open it,' he said again, close behind her.

Her fingers were trembling when they reached for the ribbon. It was store-wrapped, she noted, pulling at it so that the bow gave easily. She slid her fingers under one edge of the paper and then the next, and finally opened the slit at the back, unpeeling the gift with interest. The back of the box was white, giving no hint of what it contained. But when she turned it over it had a thick plastic window, showing cream lace.

She lifted the lid and stared inside, her lips tugging downwards.

Though the dress was folded into a neat rectangle, there could be no mistaking what Gabe had given her.

'A wedding gown?' She lifted it from the box so that she could see it at full height.

It was incredibly beautiful, just what she might have chosen for herself. Lace, long, like something from the twenties, with beads down the back and slightly off the shoulder.

But why was he giving it to her?

She bit down on her lip, turning to face him, her expression quizzical.

'You wanted to make today memorable,' he said, the words oddly lacking any emotion whatsoever. Only his dark eyes showed a hint of intensity. 'So? What do you say? Shall we get married?'

Abby stared at him, her blood rushing so fast she was sure he must hear it. 'We are getting married.'

'I mean now.'

'You mean…today?'

He laughed. 'Yes, today. Well, once Raf has had another nap perhaps,' he said as the little baby yawned in Gabe's big, strong arms. 'Will that give you enough time to get ready?'

Abby was numb. She nodded, but everything was going too fast, as if she'd inadvertently stepped into quicksand. She draped the wedding dress over a chair and when she smiled at Gabe she didn't meet his eyes.

Everything she wanted was before her, but it was a poisoned chalice. Marrying Gabe, knowing the limits of what they were—it was like being dragged beneath the ocean.

'I'll take him upstairs.' She held her arms out for Raf, the words stilted, but Gabe shook his head.

'I'll do it. You go. Start to prepare.'

Prepare? Could she ever?

'A priest will be here just after lunch,' he said

with his trademark confidence. 'Monique and Rosa will witness the wedding for us. Just as you wished.'

Abby nodded, but her whole body was resisting. Not because she didn't want to marry him, but because marrying him like this would break her.

She needed him to see that! Because if he didn't, she knew her heart would be a lifelong casualty.

But Gabe was walking away, talking in soft Italian to Raf as he carried him up the stairs. Abby watched them go, her heart sinking further. On autopilot, she lifted the dress, carrying it carefully up the stairs and into her bedroom.

Why was this turn of events so hard to process? They'd discussed the wedding several times before. She'd known he wished to marry sooner rather than later. This made sense.

She was just overthinking it—hoping for a fantasy, praying for a miracle, when she should have known better. There was no such thing, was there? Christmas notwithstanding, theirs was not a fairy tale; there was no happily ever after in store for them.

She showered, long and slow, deliciously warm, lathering herself in soap, breathing in its floral aroma. The dress was visible through the door; she tried not to look at it.

Once she had dried herself and styled her hair into an elegant chignon, she began to apply her make-up. Only halfway through, she wondered if she should have put the dress on first?

She wasn't good at this; she needed someone to help her. Someone who knew about weddings. It was probably why brides usually got ready for their weddings surrounded by their friends—their mothers.

She walked towards the dress and the moment she touched it tears welled in her eyes. Her own mother should have been with her. Or her father. Certainly some of her friends. But they'd all dropped away when her father had disowned her. Without the financial means to keep up with their lifestyle, Abby had found herself completely alone.

Now? She had a baby and a fiancé. Soon a husband. But there was no love there. She'd been wrong before to think she could make do with the sensible, practical justification for this wedding. It would be the loneliest marriage imaginable.

A sob racked her slender body and she wrapped her arms tightly around her waist.

It was useless.

She *couldn't* do this. She couldn't marry Gabe. Everything about it felt wrong; she was suffocating. Dying. Drowning.

She had to tell him how she felt. He might be angry but she couldn't let that stop her. She wouldn't marry him like this. He still hadn't forgiven her for what she'd done—and he probably never would. There was no way she could have a husband who despised her—and especially not when she loved him with all her heart.

Abby had no choice: she went in search of Gabe, certainty growing with each step. She found him in his bedroom, wearing a tuxedo that made her bones melt and her pulse race.

'You look…amazing,' she said honestly, clicking the door shut. Her breath was burning in her lungs, torturing her with every exhalation.

'Thank you.' He frowned as he took in the jeans and sweatshirt she was wearing.

'You didn't like the dress?'

'The dress is beautiful,' Abby whispered hoarsely. 'But, Gabe…' More tears moistened her eyes. 'God, Gabe, I can't… I can't marry you.'

She squeezed her eyes shut, her heart breaking into a thousand pieces.

'Abigail?' He crossed the room but didn't touch her. He was close to her though; she could feel his warmth and strength and it thawed her, just a little, but enough. She opened her eyes, dared to face him, to meet his gaze head-on.

'What's happened?'

Her expression was pinched. 'Tell me why you want to marry me.'

'You know why we're marrying,' he said with a deep frown. 'We've gone over that.'

'In New York,' she said with a shake of her head. 'That feels like a long time ago.'

His frown deepened. 'Nothing's changed since then.'

'Are you so sure of that?' she murmured.

He frowned.

'We were different people then,' she said urgently.

'In what way?'

'*I* was different,' she amended, rubbing her palms together, lost in thought. 'I was exhausted and scared, and angry and hurt. I was so, so tired. So worried about money. And I wasn't thinking clearly. I truly believed I was making the right decision in coming here with you. That I could marry you as easily as I could slip on a new winter coat or…' her eyes dropped to her hand '…an engagement ring.'

'It is easy,' he said firmly. 'We have a son together, and now we'll marry.'

'That makes it sound black and white. What about all the grey in between?'

'What grey?'

'All of this is grey,' she said emphatically. 'You were so angry with me in New York—and now? I don't know what you are. We're together at night but in the day we're like strangers in this huge castle. I can't… I just can't marry you if this is what our life would be like.'

His eyes sparked with hers, dark emotions obvious in their depths. 'I see.' The words were a grim indictment.

'You don't want to marry me either,' she pointed out with a tight grimace. 'Do you?'

'Do I strike you as a man who would do anything he didn't wish?'

'I mean if there were no Raf.'

He looked at her for several moments and then shook his head. 'I have no interest in discussing hypothetical scenarios.'

'I need to hear you say it,' she murmured. 'I need you to tell me that if it weren't for Raf…'

'Why?'

'Just tell me. If there were no Raf. If I'd never got pregnant…' She stared at him, refusing to back down, even when her breath was straining in her chest.

'Fine. If it weren't for Raf then no, we wouldn't be getting married.'

Abby's heart, so fragile, so wounded already, lurched painfully. It was the confirmation she'd needed, but now that he'd said it she had no idea how to make sense of his feelings. They were so different to hers. How had she let herself fall in love with him? Or had she really had any choice in the matter?

'I don't know why you're complicating this.'

She dug her fingernails into her palms and looked past him. 'I can't marry you if I think this is just a pragmatic decision for you. If your feelings aren't engaged at all.'

'I feel many things,' he disagreed. 'I feel a desire to do what's right for my son. I feel a desire to do what's right for you.'

Abby swept her eyes shut. She'd been wrong. Some things *were* black and white, and staying here with Gabe was one end of that extreme. It was wrong, and she was crazy not to have seen that sooner. Pain warred with certainty inside her.

'I'm not your mother, and you're not your father. We were never a great love affair. I'm not begging you to do this, and you can't change history by marrying me.' She angled her face away from him, knowing she couldn't witness the cold rejection that she presumed must be on his features. She needed to say her piece and be done with it. 'I want Raf to have a family too. Neither of us knew what that was like. But this marriage would make me miserable, Gabe. And I think you'd come to resent me—even more than you do now—if we were to go through with it.'

'I don't resent you,' he said sharply.

'Yes, you do. You resent me for Calypso. You resent me for being Lionel Howard's daughter. You resent me for having your baby. I can't live with that.'

He shook his head. 'It's not that simple.'

'Shades of grey?' she prompted, her smile without humour.

He took a step towards her, his breath an impatient exhalation. 'I understand the power your father had over you and I *understand* why you did what you did that night.'

It wasn't forgiveness. She knew he'd never trust her, never love her. His words changed nothing.

'I can't marry you.' The words were loaded with all the pain in her heart, but as she said them she knew it was the right decision. Finally, amid all this confusion, she had found her way to the truth she should have discovered earlier.

He let out a sound of pure frustration. 'What the hell do you want from me? Tell me and I'll give it to you! This marriage is worth fighting for.'

'There is no marriage,' she interjected, her temper rising.

'Fine! We won't marry today. It was just an idea. Take your time, plan the wedding you want, just…'

'Time won't change the fact that you don't love me.'

The statement surprised them both. Silence fell in the room, heavy and oppressive.

Abby looked at his face and there was such confusion there that she almost pitied him. 'I'm not marrying someone who doesn't love me. You might think it's childish, but I believe in love. I want to be with someone who adores me and that's never going to be you, is it?'

For once, Gabe was the one who seemed lost for words.

'My mother loved my father,' he said finally. 'And it killed her. I swore to myself I'd never love anyone.'

'You love Raf. You love Noah.'

His lips twisted. 'Those I couldn't help.'

She turned away from him and nodded. He didn't love her; he never would. She exhaled a shaky breath, a wave of sadness threatening to drown her. She had to be courageous—if she didn't leave him now she never would, and she'd be miserable.

'You don't love me either,' he said softly. 'That's why this marriage makes such perfect sense. We get on well enough and we both adore our son. We're great in bed together and we're intellectually well-matched. You know all about my business, courtesy of your father. This marriage has everything I want.'

Abby pressed her fist against her mouth to silence a sob. 'That sounds like a perfect recipe,' she muttered.

'I'm glad you agree.'

'I don't! I was being sarcastic! I just told you I won't marry if there's no love, and you're enumerating a sensible list for a perfectly loveless marriage. It's not what I want for my life.'

Only the sound of his breathing punctuated the air. Abby kept her back to him so she didn't see the look of visceral pain that crossed his face. Being left was nothing new to Gabe—he'd been abandoned by almost everyone his whole life. He'd kept himself closed off for a reason, and Abigail was reminding him exactly why now.

Only this wasn't just about losing Abigail.

He thought of Raf leaving the castle, Raf no longer being within arm's reach, and his whole body felt as though it had caught alight.

'Our reasons for marrying haven't changed. I want to raise my son, and I want to raise him here. If you won't stay, then we have to face the reality of a custody dispute.'

Abigail squeezed her eyes shut and when she turned to face him she was as pale as a sheet. 'Are you actually threatening to take him away from me?'

'No.' His frown deepened. 'I don't want to do that, Abigail. But he's my son and I want to be in his life.'

'You can be. That's not contingent on us marrying.'

'I want to be in his life *all the time*. I won't be a part-time father.'

'So what do you suggest?' she asked, numb all over.

'I've made my suggestion—that we get married. It seems to be the best way forward. But if you disagree, I believe it's your turn to come up with an alternative.'

She ground her teeth together. 'I won't give up my son.'

'And nor will I.' He thrust his hands on his hips. 'And when you contemplate your future, perhaps you should remember the resources I will bring to any custody battle and ask yourself whether staying here mightn't be easiest.'

She dipped her head forward, breathing in sharply, trying to inflate her lungs without success. It took several moments for the feeling of dangerous light-headedness to pass. Finally, she pinpointed him with her gaze, her eyes holding his.

'You're threatening me?'

Gabe thought about denying it, but what was the point? He was giving her an ultimatum, knowing full well what she'd choose. That knowledge sat inside him like a heavy, sharp rock, but he didn't back away. He glared at her for a long moment, ignoring the shot of pain he felt to see the hurt in her face. 'As I've said, it's your decision.'

Tears welled up in her eyes. His stomach lurched.

'I'm going to Rome for a couple of days. You can tell me what you've decided when I return.'

The phone call came early the next morning. He awoke disoriented with a banging head and a throbbing low in his gut, as though the fine blade of a knife had slid along his chest all night long.

He pushed up groggily, noting with a frown that he was in his Rome apartment.

But why?

He looked around, wincing when he saw a nearly empty bottle of Scotch with a solitary glass beside it.

Abby.

Memories of the day before came rushing back.

The way they'd argued; the things he'd said.

The threat he'd made.

Her face when he'd told her he would fight her for Raf. He didn't want to lose his son but, hell, he'd never planned to sue Abby for custody. He'd wanted his cake and to eat it too. Raf, Abby—it was all part of the same equation. He'd wanted to give Raf a family.

And what did he want?

Not this.

He felt the sentiment of what he'd said—he'd been honest with her but, God, he'd also been an ass. She was young and inexperienced and believed herself in love with him; instead of gently reminding her that everything was new and overwhelming, he'd thrown his lack of emotion at her like a trophy. His determination to not become a fool in love had always made sense, but now it seemed childish. Stupid. Pathetic, even.

He answered the phone in a rush, hope flaring inside him.

'Arantini.'

'Oh, Gabe?' The voice on the other end wasn't Abby's. His heart dropped.

'It's Holly Scott-Leigh. *Dr* Scott-Leigh,' she said. Gabe racked his brain and for one moment panic assailed him. Raf? Abby? No. This was the doctor he'd convinced Noah to see, the therapist.

God, he'd let the ball drop there. His best friend was going through hell and, apart from the occasional phone call, Gabe had been so wrapped up in his own life that he hadn't bothered to so much as think of Noah.

'Yes, Holly?' He was unintentionally curt, but he could think only of Abby.

'I'm worried about Noah,' she said, her voice trembling. 'I think he needs you. Urgently.'

It was, without a doubt, the only possible thing that could momentarily push Abby from his mind.

'Why? What's happened?'

'I… I think you should come here. To London. To see him. I'm sorry, it's just… I don't know what else to do.'

Gabe was already reaching for his jacket. 'I'll come *subito.*'

CHAPTER THIRTEEN

It was only right to pack the tree away.

How stupid she'd been to think she could decorate the house into a state of festive merriment and somehow make her heart whole when it had been obliterated into a thousand pieces.

Without Hughie, it would take all her efforts to get the thing down and drag it through the door, but she didn't care. She would do it because its very presence, two days after Christmas, was mocking her.

She unwrapped the lights with care, placing them on one of the chairs, and then, with a sense of satisfaction born purely of emotional need, she pushed at the tree until it collapsed with a loud, echoing thud to the ground. The scent of pine filled the air; she didn't breathe it in. She could barely breathe.

Gabe had been gone two nights.

Christmas night had been spent in a state of almost catatonic numbness, unable to comprehend what had happened. Boxing Day had been spent with Raf, and yet her ears had been listening for Gabe the whole time, for any sign of his approach.

There had been none. No helicopter to herald his return.

Was this how he expected their life to go? Would he just run away whenever she disagreed with him?

An angry sob burst from her and she stomped her foot, bending down and grabbing the tree by its narrower end, trying with all her might to drag it towards the door.

It didn't budge more than an inch.

She let out a roar, hoping that would help. It didn't.

But when she straightened, dragging a hand over her brow, she heard a noise behind her. The door slamming shut.

'What the hell are you doing?'

She whipped around, her eyes flashing to Gabe's with all the hurt and pain and accusation she felt before she sobered and tried to look cool. Hard to do while sweating and pink-faced from wrestling with an overgrown Christmas relic.

'What does it look like?' she snapped, refusing to let herself feel *anything* for the man, no matter how much she'd missed him, no matter how arrogantly handsome he looked.

'Abby…' He moved towards her and she flinched without realising it, backing away, closer to the tree. His eyes roamed her face and something passed between them, something that made her heart hurt and her chest thick with sobs she refused to give in to. Then he was Gabe Arantini, successful tycoon, tech billionaire. He stared at her for two more seconds before looking away, his eyes settling on a point past her shoulder. 'My plane is on the runway, refuelling now. When you're ready, I'll drive you to the airport.'

Abby froze, her chest cleaving, and fear had her launching at Gabe. 'Don't you dare! Don't you dare send me away!'

'What are you saying?' he asked, having to raise his voice to be heard above her.

'You don't want me, I get it. I don't care. I can't leave my son. I won't lose him. Don't you *dare* send me away from him! I'll marry you, I'll marry you. Just please let me stay with him.'

Gabe looked as though she'd stabbed him. He reached for her wrists and contained them with ease, his strong fingers wrapping around her, holding her tight. He spoke with urgency, his voice hoarse. 'I'm not sending you away from Raf.' His eyes were suspiciously moist, his voice gravelly. 'He'll go with you. You were right. This whole scheme was madness. We'll find another way to do this.'

Now Abby did sob because even though she'd told him she needed to be free of this whole marriage scenario, the reality was ripping her apart. Life without Gabe flashed before her, a barren, empty, hollow reality she didn't want to contemplate.

'I have an apartment in New York. You can have it. I'll buy somewhere else for myself. Do you have a lawyer?'

His fingers, curled around her wrists, were making her flesh warm yet her blood was ice-cold. 'No,' she whispered.

'Fine. You can use my lawyer too. I'll engage someone else.'

'Why do we need a lawyer? I have nothing to give you, and you've just said you'll let me be with Raf.'

His face tightened. 'I presume you won't want to deal directly with me,' he said matter-of-factly. 'We can arrange visitation rights through our lawyers. You keep the nannies and when I have Raf they'll come too, so at least there'll always be some kind of continuity for him.' He cleared his throat.

'Continuity,' she repeated, for no reason except that she couldn't understand what was happening and she had no idea how to make sense of it.

Gabe, as if just realising he was holding her, stepped backwards, dropping her arms swiftly and rubbing his palms on his jeans. 'Go and pack, Abigail. You've got your wish. You're going home.'

Her wish? Her wish was for Gabe to love her, for them to be a real family. He was showing her what he wanted—and it wasn't a life with her.

'Is this really what you want?' she whispered.

He stared at her, a strange mix of fear and determination in his eyes. 'I don't want to hurt you more than I have,' he muttered. 'You have to leave here. Go home.'

Tears welled in her eyes but she nodded. He was right. He'd never promised her anything like love. Her grief was all her own fault. She was the one who'd forgotten the parameters of their relationship. She was the one who'd fallen in love.

Without another word, she left the room. She moved through the house quickly, fighting an instinct, the whole time, to return to him. To beg him to reconsider. But that was a foolish impulse, one born of hope rather than reality. And so she forced herself to ignore it.

It didn't take Abby long to return their things to her suitcase. She'd brought only what she absolutely needed. There were clothes in New York. She would have a fresh start.

She lifted Raf out of the cot, her eyes brimming with tears as she carried him down the sweeping stairs. Gabe had removed the Christmas tree and the foyer was now empty, barren, like her heart and the marriage they might have had.

This was the right decision. She was numb, yet it was right.

But when Gabe approached her and his eyes dropped to the baby in her arms, she felt as if the earth was tipping on its axis. He stared at Raf and she saw his heartbreak, saw the cruelty of what she was doing, and grief throbbed hard in her veins.

'I can't take him away from you,' she said desperately. 'That's not right either.'

Gabe shifted his attention to Abby's face and then looked away again. 'I'll come to New York,' he said with an attempt at detachment. 'I'll see him often. You should be where you're happy.'

She swept her eyes shut, acknowledging that he was doing this for her. That he wanted to spare her pain, and so was sending her away. She acknowledged that even when her heart was breaking, both for herself and their son.

'If that's what you want,' she said, cuddling Raf close. 'Would you like to...?' She held their son towards Gabe and he made a guttural noise of pain before taking the boy from her and pulling him to his chest. He turned his back on Abby but she could see from the way his torso was moving that he was struggling to bring his own emotions under control.

She stood behind him, wishing more than anything on earth that she'd said nothing to him. That she'd simply married him and made the best of what they had. Sex, a baby they both loved and a future that could have been anything they chose. Maybe, just maybe, he'd been wrong. Maybe one day he would have learned to love her, despite what he thought now. And would that have been enough? Could she have spent her life waiting, hoping, wondering?

'Well,' he said finally. 'We should go.'

He didn't speak on the drive to the airport and nor did Abby. Every time she formulated what she wanted to say, she took one look at the determined set of his features and remembered that Gabe Arantini wasn't a man who did anything he didn't want. Gabe didn't want Abby's love. It had terrified him, and so he was disposing of her.

When they arrived at the airport he brought the car to a stop at a private terminal and turned to face her. 'Abby?'

She waited, her heart suspended, needing to hear what he was going to say, needing it with all of her being.

'I'm sorry for bringing you to Italy. When you told me about Raf, I reacted without thinking. I had no right to displace your life as I did. No right to manipulate you into an engagement that was so obviously wrong.'

She bit down on her lip and her huge eyes held his for several devastating moments. 'I'm sorry I fell in love with you,' she said softly.

He shook his head and reached for her cheek, cupping it with his hand. 'Don't be. I don't deserve your love—I don't want it—but that doesn't mean it's not an incredible...privilege.'

She sobbed then, because it made no sense and

because she wanted him to understand something she couldn't even explain.

'Text me when you land,' he said, pulling away from her and opening his door. He came around to her side and opened it before returning to the rear of the car and removing Raf. 'And if you need anything. Anything at all.' His eyes burned her with their intensity; Abby could no longer look at Gabe.

It hurt too soul-destroyingly much.

It was her engagement ring that did it.

He found it on her side of his bed—not that she'd ever used the bed as her own. She'd come to him each night and they'd made love, but she'd acted like a guest in his room. A guest in his castle, and his life.

He lay on his back, staring at the ceiling, but it was no good. The bed smelled of her, of them. He swore sharply and sat up straight, rubbing his eyes with the palms of his hands. It hadn't even been a week—how was he meant to do this?

Every time he closed his eyes he saw her as she'd been at the airport. Her face so pale, clutching Raf. His child, and the mother of his child, boarding a flight to take them halfway across the world.

He'd sat in his car and watched the plane lift off, imagining them settling in for the flight, wondering if Abigail was nervous or relieved? Relieved to be leaving him, relieved to be free of his threats and control?

He groaned and stood, pacing out of his room towards his study. He poured himself a measure of Scotch but cradled the glass in his hand, looking at the door against which they'd made love.

A glimmer of hope flashed in his belly. She'd been worried about falling pregnant. Might she have? Might she, even now, have his baby in her belly? Would that change her mind? Surely then she'd marry him?

With rich self-disgust he threw the Scotch back, burning his mouth with the alcoholic acidity. Was he really so desperate to secure his family that he'd wish her to be pregnant when she so obviously hadn't wanted that? Was he such a despicable man?

She'd called him honourable; she'd been wrong.

He'd ruined Abigail's life. She'd given him the chance to be involved with their baby; she'd needed his help. Help he could have given to her easily. He *should* have given it to her. When he'd seen the way she was living, and comprehended how alone she was in the world, he could have made everything better. Instead, he'd strong-armed her into agreeing to marriage and moving to Italy, and all because it suited him to have her here.

And yet the thing that terrified Gabe most of all was the certainty that he would do it all again, simply because he knew that at each step of the way he'd been desperate for whatever he could get of her.

It had started as hate, hadn't it? Maybe even revenge?

No. Never revenge. Just…inexplicable, all-controlling desire. Something heavy sat low in his gut. He'd wanted her. He'd seen her in New York and after a year without women—no, not *women*— a year without *Abigail* specifically, he'd lost his mind. He'd been determined to make her his once more. So why had he treated her as he had? Why had he embarrassed her at work, and told Rémy to fire her? Why hadn't he let her explain properly— all the words he knew she needed to say, and had told her he didn't want to hear, even when he'd been aching for her to give him something that would eradicate the pain of her betrayal?

But it hadn't really been a betrayal. Oh, she'd come to him intending to steal Calypso's secrets, but it was out of desperation and love for her father. Knowing Abigail as he did now, he didn't doubt her version of events. She would never have gone through with it.

But he would have.

He would have married her on Christmas Day knowing that it was a last resort for her. Knowing she was standing there, pledging her life and heart to him purely because he'd presented her with that sole option.

He'd been trying to prove that he was nothing like his father; instead, he was so very much worse. He'd been terrified of losing Abigail and yet he hadn't realised until now—until it was too late.

With a hoarse oath, he pitched the Scotch glass at the wall so that it cracked into several pieces and hit the ground with a splintering shriek.

He was terrified of losing Abigail and so he'd lost her.

CHAPTER FOURTEEN

GABE STOOD OUTSIDE the door to his Manhattan penthouse for so long he wondered if, in the week since seeing Abigail, he'd become some kind of madman. It was his home—at least it had been until she'd left Italy. He felt as though a nest of snakes was writhing in his chest cavity.

He clutched the soft toy he'd bought for Raf in one hand and lifted the other to the door and knocked. Twice. Loud. Confident. Nothing that betrayed the way his stomach was twisting and his mind was spinning.

It wasn't until she pulled the door inwards that he realised how late it was. He winced at the sight of her—so beautiful, so sleepy, her long hair pulled over one shoulder, the oversized T-shirt she was sleeping in showing more leg than was helpful in that moment, for he needed to keep a clear mind.

'Gabe?' She blinked and rubbed her palms over her eyes.

'It's late, I'm sorry,' he said, shaking his head. 'Were you asleep?'

It was a stupid question—he could see quite clearly that she had been.

'What are you doing here?' She didn't invite him in. There was a wariness to her, a fear that he'd put there. At one time he might have pushed inside anyway, just as he had on the night he'd discovered Raf. But Gabe was done steamrollering Abby into submission. All along he'd been so wrong.

'Abigail.' The word came out as a hoarse plea. He cleared his throat and tried again. 'I need to speak with you.'

'Now?' She swallowed, her throat shifting, her vulnerability making him ache.

'I…can come back in the morning, if that's better?'

His contrition obviously confused her. She frowned, blinked her big eyes and then stepped backwards, gesturing for him to come inside.

He did so quickly, before she could change her mind, shrugging out of his suit jacket and discarding it carelessly over the back of a chair. 'This is for Raf,' he said needlessly, holding up the little monkey toy.

She crossed her arms over her chest. 'He's sleeping. If you wanted to see him.' She angled her face away from him and he wanted to shout, *No!*, because he needed to see her, to study her, but he didn't. Instead, he clenched his hand into a fist by his side, urging himself to be patient, to be gentle. To respect her autonomy and to respect the fact she'd probably tell him to go to hell—with good reason.

'I do, of course.' He nodded. 'But I meant what I said. I need to speak to you.'

She frowned. 'Is everything okay? Are you sick? Is it Noah?'

His chest crushed. Why hadn't he noticed the level of her compassion before? Why hadn't he understood that she was full of care for others—which in part had led to her downfall? It was compassion for Lionel that had sent her to Gabe, and compassion for Raf that had brought her to Italy.

'I'm fine.' He didn't mention Noah. It was early days there and he was keeping a close eye on the situation.

'Good.' She stepped away from him, towards the kitchen. 'Would you like anything? Coffee?'

He shook his head but followed her, watching as she poured herself water and took a small sip.

'How are you?'

'Fine,' she said, but her eyes shifted away from him and he ached for her, for the obvious hurt he'd inflicted.

'I thought that if I married you I'd be a better man than my father. But it turns out I'm every bit as bad. Worse, actually.'

Her eyes lifted to his face and she said nothing, waiting for him to continue.

'I told myself it was right for all of us; the best thing we could do for our son. But I ignored your feelings and needs. I should have helped you to live a better life here, in New York, but I was self-ish. I wanted you in Italy and so I bullied you into coming there with me. I treated you so much worse than I accused your father of doing. How you didn't scratch my eyes out is beyond me.'

She shook her head but he couldn't let her interrupt. What if she told him to leave? He needed to at least say what he'd come to tell her, and then let her decide what she wanted. And he would need to respect that decision.

'When I got back to Italy, after Christmas, I just knew I couldn't be responsible for making you miserable. All I could think about was the way you looked when we argued. The things I said. The way you stared at me as though I was…' He shook his head angrily, dragging his fingers through his hair. 'You were falling apart. You hated living with me; you hated Italy. I had to send you here because I wanted you to be happy. Are you happy, *tempesta*?'

Her eyes locked onto his for several long seconds and then she blinked, looking away hurriedly. 'I'm getting there.'

'I don't believe you.'

Her smile was miserable. 'That seems to be our problem. You never have believed me.'

His gut twisted sharply. 'No.' Regret made the word heavy. He ran his palm along the back of his neck, feeling the coarse hairs there.

'On Christmas Day you asked me if I loved you and I said no. I've never been in love. I've never been loved. But I've been lonely and I've been alone. I've been miserable. Most of my life was that. And then I met you.'

Abby was very still, waiting, her breath held, needing to hear something that would lift the weight that had lodged permanently on her chest.

'That night, last Christmas, my God, if you knew how I felt. How I wanted you. How I fell for you.' He swore softly under his breath. 'It was my fault that the Calypso debacle cut me to the quick. For the first time in my life, I let my guard down. I let you in. I wanted every single piece of you. Not just your body—all of you. I've never felt that way before.'

'And I lied to you,' she muttered.

'You lied to me,' he confirmed grimly. 'And I couldn't forgive you for that. But nor could I forget you.'

Only the sound of Abby's laboured breath filled the room.

'I spent a year proving to myself that I was over you and then, the whole time I was in New York, I looked for you.' He grimaced. 'I don't mean I actually tried to find you. Just that my eyes were always scanning, hoping to catch a glimpse of you. Seeing you at the restaurant was an accident, but I don't think I would have left the city without you. One way or another.'

'Don't say that,' she said with a shake of her head. 'You don't need to pretend.'

'I spent a year waiting for you. I told myself I was busy, that I was angry, but I didn't so much as look at another woman.'

Abby's stomach swirled. Disbelief warred with pleasure at his admission.

'I've spent a long time pushing people away, *tempesta*. All my life. And then you came to Italy and I relaxed, because I had everything I needed. You were living with me. You were my lover, and we had a child. I had a family. But I didn't realise how much that would hurt you. How much I was hurting you.'

'And so you let me go,' she said with a soft nod. 'I've worked that much out, Gabe. I know why you ended it. Why you sent me home. It was very *kind* of you.'

'No,' he said with a shake of his head. 'You don't understand. It wasn't because I didn't want you to stay.'

'You didn't want to hurt me,' she said, her smile one of sadness. 'You're a good person. Too good to lie to me, too good to use me.'

'I didn't want to hurt you so I sent you here, as though I could click my fingers and take us back in time. As though by sending you home I wouldn't feel like I had been hollowed out, like all of me had been dug from my body at the same time you left. I didn't want to hurt you but I didn't have any idea how much it would hurt to see you go. I've pushed people away all my life, and it comes easier to me than anything else. Even more so than admitting how I feel.'

Abby squeezed her fingernails into her palm and forced herself to face him. 'And?' she asked, the word a thin breath. 'How do you feel?'

'I feel like I have stepped into a strange world with only sharp edges and darkness. I feel like I am sinking all the time, my lungs filling with water rather than air and with no way to breathe. I wake each morning and reach for you, craving you, and then I remember. You're gone. You're here.'

'Are you saying…are you trying to say that you love me?' she demanded, hope an uncontainable beast in her breast.

'I know nothing of love,' he admitted, the words gravelly. 'What I am saying is that you are the beginning and end of my life. That without you everything is unbearable. I want to wake up and see you every morning, and hold you tight every night. I am saying that even if there were no Raf I would want you. I've spent my whole life pushing people away and I won't do it now—I can't. I want to do the opposite. I want to pull you close, to hold you near, to make you mine for the rest of my life, even when knowing how much I need you, how much power you have over me, terrifies me. *Tempesta,* you have run like a cyclone through all of me so that I'm not the same man I was the night we met. That man thought people—thought you—were disposable. I was so wrong. So very, very wrong. If you'll forgive me for being so stupid, I will make you love me too.'

And it was so ferociously determined that she laughed, a little unsteadily given that her chest was squeezing painfully.

'You're telling me you love me and still somehow doing it in a way that would control a room full of executives.'

'Apparently, I can't help doing that,' he said with a shake of his head. 'It makes what I say no less true.'

'Gabe—' she kept her distance '—I know enough of your upbringing to know how much loyalty means to you. Trust too. How will you ever trust me after what you found me doing?' Her cheeks flamed. 'You've told me again and again that you don't believe me. That you think I was unequivocally going to give those images to my father. There's no hope for us when you feel as you do. I've spent a long time coming to terms with that.'

'And so have I. I cannot live without you, and

I unequivocally believe what you said.' He shook his head angrily. 'I *do* believe you. I cannot explain it. The rational part of my brain demands proof and explanations, but the part of me that knows you, that understands you, simply *believes*.' He took a step towards her and when she didn't step backwards he lifted his hands and cupped her face. 'You know almost as much about rejection and loneliness as I do.' His gaze bored into hers, seeing all the secrets of her soul. 'Your mother died and you were abandoned. Your father shut you out at every opportunity. Is it any wonder you were prepared to do anything he asked of you? In the hopes that maybe, just maybe, that might be the thing that would make him love you?'

She sobbed and shut her eyes, his interrogation, his understanding, all too much to cope with.

'He was wrong not to see your true value. But I was more so. You gave me everything—you made me feel alive and real for the first time in years. You gave me your beautiful, kind heart and I shouted at you. I practically threatened to take your son from you.' The words were loaded with anger, all directed at himself. 'Believe me, if I could take that day back, I would. With all that I am, I wish I hadn't said those things to you. I wish I hadn't given you any reason to feel pain.'

'This is about Raf,' she whispered. 'It has to be.'

For she couldn't make sense of what was happening. All her dreams were coming true before her and she wasn't sure they were strong enough to hold her weight. 'You miss him.'

'*Sì*. I do miss Raf, but I'm as prepared now as I was a week ago to leave him with you, if that's what you want,' he insisted gently. 'This, right now, is about *you*. It's about the woman I fell in love with last Christmas, and somehow found my way to again. It's about the woman who gave me her innocence, who'd been waiting for me all her life, just as I had been waiting for her. It's about the woman who took a broken, angry man and made him smile once more. It's about the woman who has come to mean everything to me, who I do not wish to live without.' He ran his thumb over her lower lip and she juddered, her breath escaping her slowly, brushing over his inner wrist.

'I've trained myself not to want love. It's never been offered to me anyway.' He dropped his head so that their foreheads were touching and Abby breathed in deeply, letting his proximity chase the grief from her veins.

'I offered you love,' she whispered. 'I loved you every day we were in Italy. Even when I was so mad I could burst, I loved you… I wanted our marriage to be a real one,' she said. 'I felt so close to having everything I'd ever dreamed of. It was so magical—such a magical Christmas—with the snow, and the tree, and you and then the wedding dress…'

'From the moment we met, you have been all I've wanted. I've been stupid enough to run from that, but now I'm running right towards you. I want you, all of you, and if there were no Raf I would still be here, begging you, as a man who loves a woman more than any ever has, to marry me. To spend the rest of your life with me, letting me love you…'

Abby sobbed, a sound of pure, exquisite joy.

'You're going to marry me,' he said into her mouth and she nodded, laughing, before kissing him again.

'Can we go home now?'

He pulled away so he could study her face, see the earnestness there. 'Home? Where is our home to be?'

'The castle, obviously.'

His smile was the most beautiful thing she'd ever seen. 'Ah. And so it is, *mi amore.*'

EPILOGUE

'RAF!' A LITTLE girl's voice squealed with delight and when Abby turned around she saw Ivy, Noah's adopted daughter, giggling in response to Raf's attempts to grab her hair. As a two-year-old, he was charming and spirited. Abby was grateful they'd retained Monique to help chase after him!

Abby walked towards the pair of children and crouched down, lifting a manicured nail to her son's nose. 'Stop that, Rafael.' She suppressed a smile when his chubby face turned towards her. 'Ivy's mommy has spent far too long braiding her hair to have it undone by the likes of you. Now, where's your bouquet, Ivy?'

'I've got it!' Holly called from the doorway, carrying three bunches of flowers and wearing a broad smile on her beautiful face. She was glowing, but Abby had known Holly almost a year and knew it had little to do with her pregnancy. Holly was one of those women who always glowed. She was warm and kind and, from the moment they'd met—the Christmas after they'd become engaged—Abby had known they would be friends.

It had proved to be so, and the proximity of Italy and England had meant that both families met quite often.

Families.

Abby turned to her reflection in the mirror, studying the bridal gown. It was the same one Gabe had chosen and given her two years earlier, a Christmas morning that was snowy and magical, just like this one. Except not like this one because she'd been so insecure then, so uncertain of her future and what her marriage would look like. Now, every day was a gift, boxed in so much security and love that she felt as though she were floating through life.

Families.

She'd been alone for so long and now she had Raf and Gabe, and Noah, Holly and Ivy, and Holly's big, chaotic extended family too.

'Your father's outside,' Holly said softly, handing a small box to Abby. 'And the groom asked me to give you this.'

Abby took the box and opened it, her fingers shaking a little at the mention of her father.

It was a big step for him to have come to Italy— and that was all down to Gabe's persistence. It was the reason they'd waited two years to marry. He'd understood, without needing to be told, how much it would mean to Abby to have her father walk her down the aisle at her wedding.

Irrespective of Lionel Howard's sins, he was the only family from her old life that she had left and she wasn't ready to shut the door on that completely. So Gabe had made it his mission to smooth the fractures of their relationship. It had been disastrous at first, but Gabe was not a man to take no for an answer, and by the following Christmas a fragile truce had been formed.

Now, a year later, it was still fragile, still young, but Abby was glad that there was the prospect of a future that included her father. If he chose not to make the most of it, then she'd accept that. She'd let him go, knowing that what she and Gabe had was special, that he could be a part of it if he wanted, but that you couldn't force love. You couldn't force someone to want you.

'What's in the box, Abby?' Ivy asked, coming to stand beside her.

'Let's find out, shall we?' She unwrapped it and lifted the lid, tears moistening her eyes when she saw the decoration inside.

'What is it?' Ivy asked again.

'It's a tradition,' Abby whispered, then smiled brightly, lifting the decoration so Ivy and Holly could see the delicate etchings on each side. It was of the castle, she realised, a single tear running down her cheek.

'Stop that!' Holly said with a laugh, dabbing at it with a tissue. 'You'll ruin your make-up.'

'Why do we cry when we're happy?' Abby asked with a laugh. 'Because I am. Happier than I ever thought I'd be.'

'Just about as happy as you deserve, I'd say,' Holly said kindly, running a palm over her rounded tummy. 'Shall I get your father?'

Abby sucked in a deep breath and nodded. 'Yes. I'm ready.'

'Come on, you two.' Holly held her hands out to the children and guided them from the room. Abby wasn't alone for long. A moment later, Lionel walked in, his expression guarded until he looked at his daughter, properly looked at her, and then was arrested where he stood, unable to keep walking.

'You look…' He shook his head. 'You are so like her,' he said slowly.

Abby ignored the twisting of her heart, the pain that came from knowing she would always be just a reflection of her mother to him. It was enough that he was there—not because she wouldn't have been happy to marry without her father's presence, but because it was yet another proof of the myriad ways in which Gabe loved her. There had been many testaments to that fact over the two years since they'd become engaged, and each reminder of how special she was to him filled her with a rush of pleasure.

'Shall we?'

Lionel nodded, holding his arm out for Abby. She put her hand in the crook of his arm, took one last look at herself and smiled. 'Let's go then.'

They walked towards the stairs of the castle, but at the top, before they came into view of the wedding guests, he paused, turning to face his daughter, a frown on his face.

It was natural for Abby to experience a jolt of anxiety. She didn't want her father to be there to only ruin the day. She waited, her breath held, for what he would say.

'I do love you, Abby. I know I'm not a good father. After your mother died I just couldn't be anything to anyone.' He shook his head. 'My business was everything. I look at you now and I realise I don't know anything about the young woman you've become.'

Abby expelled a sigh of relief. 'There's time to get to know me, Dad. Our door is open to you.'

And tears sparkled in his eyes as he shook his head. 'That's better than I deserve.'

Abby tilted her head. 'Yes,' she agreed with a teasing smile—the smile of a woman so completely in love and content that nothing could bring her down for long.

They began to walk once more, and halfway down the stairs the makeshift wedding venue came into sight. The foyer had been decorated with another huge tree—their third in the castle—and seats had been set to view it. She couldn't see her groom yet, though. That moment was reserved for when she and Lionel reached the ground floor and moved forward.

Then Abby's heart jolted in recognition of her mate, her partner, her purpose.

He stood, tall and handsome, in front of the tree, dressed in a jet-black tuxedo with a crisp white shirt, but it was his eyes that almost felled her. They were boring into her with the intensity that was part and parcel of his love for her.

She smiled at him, a smile of love, of understanding. As the music began to play she walked down the aisle with her father.

Noah stood beside Gabe and, as they got close, Gabe turned to his best friend and nodded at something Noah said. Noah turned to look at his own wife before patting Gabe on the back.

Later, after the ceremony, when they were dancing at the reception, their guests surrounding them with happiness and love, Abby asked her husband what Noah had said.

'He said we've done it.' Gabe grinned.

'Done what?'

'Outgrown our childhoods.' And for a second he frowned, but it was the work of an instant, then he was her Gabe once more, self-assured, arrogant, perfect.

She lifted onto tiptoe and kissed his lips softly. She would spend the rest of her life trying to erase the pain of his upbringing. Starting now.

'I sometimes find it hard to imagine Noah ever being like you described. He's so strong, like you.'

'He'd been badly hurt,' Gabe said quietly. 'And often. There aren't many people who could weather what he did...'

Gabe and Abby looked towards their friends, studying their obvious intimacy, their perfect partnership. Ivy was nearby, dancing with another friend of Gabe's, standing on the man's shoes, laughing at the jokes he was telling.

'Holly is glowing,' Abby murmured, tilting her head to look at her friend. She danced close to Noah, and she smiled at them. Noah was so like Gabe. Despite the fact they weren't biologically related, there was a similar spirit to both men. A strength and honour that ran through both. Little wonder they'd found one another and clung on in the midst of everything they'd lost.

'She is.' He nodded.

'I'm pleased for them. Another baby will certainly keep Ivy busy.'

'And save Raf from her mothering,' Gabe agreed with a laugh.

Abby grinned. He was right. Ivy adored Raf and spent most of their time together chasing after him, 'helping' him in every way.

'She'll be a great big sister,' Abby said thoughtfully.

'True.'

'And Raf? Do you think he'll make a good big brother?'

'I have no doubt he would.' He stared at her, a frown on his face as he tried to interpret her meaning. 'You'd like another baby?'

'Yes. In fact…'

He stopped dancing, holding her close. 'You're pregnant?'

'Yes.'

'You're pregnant!' His face wore a mask of such pleasure that Abby felt her eyes moisten once more. Happy tears seemed to be all she had left these days.

'I'm twelve weeks. I hope you don't mind that I didn't tell you. I wanted it to be your Christmas present.'

'Mind? It's the best Christmas gift you could have arranged.'

'Well, you helped with the arrangement,' she pointed out with a blush.

Gabe laughed, his eyes shining with passion, but then he sobered, pressing his finger to her chin and lifting her face so their eyes latched. 'I'm going to be with you this time, Abby. I'm going to be by your side for everything.'

She placed her head against his chest so she could hear the solid, reliable beating of his heart and there was truth in every drum.

'I'm going to be with you for it all, and for every

day afterwards, my beautiful, irreplaceable *tempesta*. And all the Christmases of our lives.'

She smiled and swept her eyes shut, wondering if when she opened them again this would all turn out to be a dream. For how could reality be so utterly perfect? She blinked and he was there. So were their friends. Everybody as happy as before, everything as perfect as she could wish.

Outside the castle, snow began to drift downwards—the icing on the cake of their perfect Christmas miracle.

* * * * *

If you enjoyed
Bound by Their Christmas Baby
look out for the first instalment in
Clare Connelly's
Christmas Seductions duet!

The Season to Sin

Available in Harlequin Dare